I0640835

John Martin Routh

The Law of Artistic Copyright

A handy book for the use of artists, publishers, and photographers - With

explanatory dialogues

John Martin Routh

The Law of Artistic Copyright
A handy book for the use of artists, publishers, and photographers - With explanatory dialogues

ISBN/EAN: 9783337406103

Printed in Europe, USA, Canada, Australia, Japan

Cover: Foto ©Andreas Hilbeck / pixelio.de

More available books at **www.hansebooks.com**

THE LAW OF ARTISTIC COPYRIGHT.

A HANDY BOOK FOR THE USE OF
ARTISTS, PUBLISHERS AND PHOTOGRAPHERS.

WITH EXPLANATORY DIALOGUES.

BY

MARTIN ROUTH,

Of the Inner Temple, Barrister-at-Law.

𝕷𝖔𝖓𝖉𝖔𝖓:

REMINGTON AND CO.,

NEW BOND STREET, W.

—

1881.

To

HEYWOOD   HARDY,   ESQ.,

At whose suggestion a practical explanation of the working

of the Copyright Statutes, in relation to works of art was

attempted, this book is affectionately inscribed by the

AUTHOR.

April, 1881.

CONTENTS.

CHAPTER IV.

DIALOGUE ON PHOTOGRAPHY.

CHAPTER V.

COPYRIGHT IN ENGRAVINGS, ETCHINGS, AND LITHOGRAPHS.

CHAPTER VI.

PIRACY OF ENGRAVINGS, ETCHINGS, AND LITHOGRAPHS.

CHAPTER VII.

COPYRIGHT IN PAINTINGS, DRAWINGS, AND PHOTOGRAPHS.

CHAPTER VIII.

PIRACY OF PAINTINGS, DRAWINGS, AND PHOTOGRAPHS.

CHAPTER IX.

COPYRIGHT IN SCULPTURE, BUSTS, MODELS, &C.

CHAPTER X.

INTERNATIONAL COPYRIGHT.

CHAPTER XI.

THE STATUTE OF FRAUDS.

APPENDIX.

TABLE OF CASES ·CITED.

INTRODUCTION.

It is not the object of this little work to enter into a lengthy discussion on the respective rights of the public and of the artist in a property which is exclusively the creation of the genius of the latter. The purpose is rather to try and explain the compromise between them by which they are at present bound, and which is known as Artistic Copyright. Artists are unanimous in thinking that in the making of this compromise they have been hardly treated by the Legislature. "Copyright," they complain, "should be ours until we part with it." The answer of the Copyright Commissioners is as follows :—"The evidence shows that persons buying pictures do not in general think about the copyright, but that if the subject happens to be mentioned they are generally under the impression that the copyright is included in the purchase,. and are astonished if they are told that it is not. It is said that owing to this fact an artist, however eminent, when he is selling a picture, shrinks from mentioning the copyright and asking for an agreement to enable him to retain it ; he usually prefers that the copyright should be lost to both parties, as in the absence of any written agreement it would be, than that the purchaser should think that he is losing a valuable part of his bargain, and consequently should decline to complete the purchase. The principal reason why artists wish to retain the copyright is to keep control over the engraver and photographer. To artists this control is a matter of considerable pecuniary value,

B

but they urge that they not only wish to control engraving in order to get the payment from the engraver,* but chiefly to prevent inferior engraving, which they consider prejudicial to their reputation. It is admitted that if a picture is sold the artist would have no power to get it engraved when it is in the possession of the purchaser except by his consent, and artists are willing that this should continue to be the case; but if this power of preventing engraving is so valuable, it is not easy to see why they should hesitate to explain the law to the purchaser, and offer to let him have the copyright, if he will preserve the picture from inferior engraving, rather than let the copyright be lost both to artist and purchaser." They then recommend an alteration in the law to the effect that in the absence of a written agreement to the contrary the copyright in a picture should belong to the purchaser, and follow the ownership of the picture.

With due respect and deference to the opinion of the majority of the Commissioners, I cannot adopt either their argument or their conclusion. There is something in natural justice which tells us that if a man elaborates from his brain a work of art, he has, by an inherent right, acquired a property in it. This property, which is the right of reproduction of the design as distinct from the original work, has now become a recognised and legalised property, and one which is often of more value than the original itself. To which of two persons should this second property in all justice belong?—to the purchaser of the work, which is nothing more than a single copy or expression of the design or abstract conception in the artist's mind, and which he can reproduce at will, or to the artist, whose genius has created the design? At present the law is that it belongs to neither without the intervention of a written agreement vesting it in one of them. That this state of things is a blot in our law, which must be remedied in any future legislation on the subject, is conceded by every one. The only question which remains is whether copyright is

* It may be supposed that the Commissioners meant " publisher."

to vest in the artist or the purchaser. It is submitted that as both properties owe their existence to the artist, they ought to remain his until he parts with them. Yet the Commissioners recommend that in parting with the one he should dispossess himself of the other, chiefly on the ground, it would seem, that a purchaser does not think about copyright at all, or, if the subject is called to his attention, is astonished that it does not belong to him! The purchaser here alluded to is, of course, the unprofessional purchaser. The dealer and the publisher, who know what copyright is, and who are, under ordinary circumstances, the only persons, other than the artist, to whom it is of the slightest pecuniary value, are willing that it should remain with the artist. This is proved by the evidence brought before the Royal Commission.

One more observation on the Commissioners' report of 1878. They ask why the artist should hesitate to explain the law as it stands to a purchaser. This presupposes a knowledge of the law which the artist does not possess. To assist him to master the law sufficiently to give such an explanation to an intending purchaser, and to protect his own interests, some dialogues have been written, which it is hoped will be found to contain answers to most of the questions likely to arise in practice.

In conclusion, the Author has availed himself of portions of the digest of the copyright law made for the Royal Commission by one of its members, Mr. Justice Stephen—then Sir James Stephen, Q.C.—whose masterly clearness in expounding the intricate statutes recommends itself to lawyers and the public alike. The Author's thanks are also due to Mr. Basil Field, of the firm of Field, Roscoe, and Co., Solicitors, whose zealous services in the cause of the artists are well known, and to Mr. J. W. Comyns Carr, for the practical hints which they have given him, and for the interest which they have shown in his work.

Temple, May, 1881.

THE LAW OF ARTISTIC COPYRIGHT.

CHAPTER I.

OF THE RIGHT OF THE OWNER AT COMMON LAW.

COPYRIGHT, in its strictly legal sense, of which it is the object of this work to treat, is the sole and exclusive right of multiplying copies of an original work after it has been published ; and the word, thus defined, must not be confounded with the other loose sense in which it is often used—viz., the right of the owner to publish in part, or wholly, or to prevent others from publishing, a work, or copies of a work, not yet published.

An artist who paints a picture has an undoubted and undisputed right to the canvas upon which the picture has been painted. He may, if he is so minded, withhold it absolutely from the view of others, or may proceed against any person who has surreptitiously copied it ; he has also a right to any copies of the picture he may make, either by engraving, etching, or by any other process, for himself or for private circulation amongst his friends. He may lend the picture to others, and annex any condition he pleases to the loan ; the fulfilment of those conditions he may proceed to enforce, and for their breach he may claim compensation. If he sells his picture the purchaser has the same right. But when once the picture has been published this right, this Common Law right of his, is gone,* and unless

* Jeffreys and Boosey, 4 H. & C. 920.

he has secured copyright by statute or copyright after publication, in substitution of the old right, the picture becomes
the property of the nation, so far as the right to reproduce
the design is concerned—a prey to the base crowd of
imitators ever on the watch to make money out of the
work of others.

Copyright after publication is thus the creature of
statute, and must, therefore, be secured by the means laid
down by the particular statutes relating to the various
works of art.

The publication of a work of art for a special and
limited purpose, upon any contract or upon a trust expressed
or implied, does not authorise the person to whom such
thing is published to copy or reproduce it, except to the
extent and for the purpose for which it has been lent or
entrusted to him.

If an artist lends his painting to a photographer to make
one or two copies from the negative for the artist's own use,
the photographer can never make any other use of the negative,* and this quite apart from the question of copyright law.
The rights of owners of unpublished works are well defined
by the case of Prince Albert v. Strange.† It appeared
from the Bill that Her Majesty the Queen and the plaintiff
had occasionally, for their amusement, made drawings and
etchings, principally of subjects of private and domestic
interest, of which etchings they had made impressions for
their own use, and not for publication. A very few of
these impressions had been distributed among the friends
of Her Majesty and the plaintiff. For greater privacy,
these impressions had, for the most part, been made by
means of a private press, and the plates themselves had
been ordinarily kept by Her Majesty under lock. Certain
of the plates were, however, given to a printer in order
that he might print off some impressions for Her Majesty.
The printer employed one Middleton, who, without the
printer's knowledge, and in violation of the confidence

* Mayall v. Higby, 1 H. & C. 148.
† 18 L.J. N.S.Ch. 120. 1 Mac. & Gor. 25.

reposed in him, took impressions for himself, and one of the defendants bought, or in some manner obtained them, from Middleton. The defendants had thereby been enabled to form, and had formed, a gallery of etchings of which they intended to make a public exhibition against the will of Her Majesty and the plaintiff. The defendants had also compiled a catalogue of the etchings to be contained in the gallery.

An injunction having been granted to restrain both the exhibition and the publication of the catalogue, upon an application to dissolve the injunction so far as related to the catalogue, Lord Chancellor Cottenham said: "The right of the plaintiff to an injunction restraining the defendant from exhibiting, copying, or in any manner publishing or parting with or disposing of any of the etchings in question is perfectly clear. . . . . The property in an author or composer of any work, whether of literature, art, or science, such work being unpublished and kept for his own use or pleasure, cannot be disputed; and it being admitted that the defendant could not publish a copy, that is an impression, of the etchings, how in principle does a catalogue list or description differ? A copy or impression of the etchings could only be a means of communicating knowledge and information of the original, and does not a list and description do the same? The means are different, but the object and effect are similar, for in both the object and effect is to make known to the public, more or less, the unpublished works and compositions of the author which he is entitled to keep wholly for his private use and pleasure, and to withhold altogether, or so far as he may please, from the knowledge of others."

Where copyright-after-publication has been lost through non-compliance with the statute, or where copyright has not been registered before the piracy complained of, it will be material to discover whether or not the work has been published, for if so, the owner of the work has, as before stated, no right of veto on its reproduction.

It is difficult to say what amounts to a publication of a

work of art, and the question in most cases must be answered with reference to the exact history of the work.

It has already been shown by Prince Albert's case, that the publication of a work for private purposes and private circulation, or the gift of a limited number of copies to friends, is not a publication.

Neither does the exhibition of a picture for the purpose of obtaining subscribers to an engraving of it amount to a publication, for it would defeat the very object for which the picture was exhibited.*

The sale of a picture is not a publication of it. The publication of a wood engraving of a painting in a magazine, with an article describing the painting, is not a publication, of the painting, for to constitute a publication there must be publication of the thing itself, and not of a copy; so the publication of a bust is not the publication of the statue from which the bust is taken.*

The exhibition of a work of art at a public exhibition or gallery is a publication, unless there are express rules and regulations of the exhibition prohibiting copying. Thus, a painting exhibited in the National Gallery, where there are no rules to prevent copying, is a published painting. On one occasion a publisher wished to prevent Turner's "Temeraire" (in the National Gallery) from being copied, but he was told that the Trustees knew of no restriction whatever, and that if he had any peculiar rights he would have to establish them in a court of law.

This took place before the existence of copyright after publication in a painting—viz., prior to the passing of the Fine Arts Act of 1862. Of course if a publisher had secured copyright in a painting now on view in the Gallery he would be able to restrain any copying or reproduction of it. It is believed to be the fact that the Trustees now refuse permission to copy any paintings or other works of art in which copyright exists.

The exhibition of a painting or other work of art in the Royal Academy does not amount to a publication, the

* Turner v. Robinson, 10 Ir. Ch. Rep., 510.

rules of the exhibition being so framed as to prohibit copying even by the artist himself.   Permission was refused to Mr. Cruikshank, who desired to copy one of his own pictures, and also to E. M. Ward, R.A., to have a copy made of his " Marie Antoinette" during exhibition.

Copyright cannot exist in immoral, irreligious, seditious, or libellous works of art, of whatever description they may be; and if a person were to destroy such a picture, print, or engraving he would be liable for nothing more than the damage done to the paper or canvas on which it was depicted.*

---

* Dubost v. Beresford, 2 Camp. 511.   Stockdale v. Onwhyn, 5 B. & C., 173.

CHAPTER II.

DIALOGUE.

Let the reader imagine an artist's studio, in which there is a painting in oil for sale. The following conversation may be supposed to take place between A., *the artist, and* B., *an intending purchaser :—*

B. : What is the price of that picture?

A. : £—.

B. : I will buy it.

A. : I reserve the copyright.

B. : But that goes with the picture, does it not?

A. : Only in the case of commissioned work, which this is not. The Act * says that if there is no written agreement signed by the purchaser vesting the copyright in the artist, or by the artist, or by his agent authorised in writing, vesting the copyright in the purchaser, at the time of the first sale, and before the transaction is completed, the copyright falls to the ground, and is irredeemably lost. In such a case any one who obtains access to the picture could pirate it in any way he pleased. I, therefore, must request you to sign this document (Form 1 †), which will vest the copyright in me, before I deliver you the picture.

B. : But I do not care for half a picture; I want the whole thing or nothing at all. Not that I have any particular use for the copyright myself, but I don't want any interference on the part of any one in my property.

A. : What you appear to want is a picture and a half; but you forget that the copyright is a distinctive and valuable property, recognised by the law, which at present belongs to me. Yet you express no desire to buy it as such. At

* 25 & 26 Vic., c. 68, s. 1.   † See Appendix.

the same time, you refuse to comply with a form which will enable me to retain what ought to be, and is, my own. Such a property ought surely to be secured to one of us, and not be thrown to the winds. It is the old story over again, and you are no exception to the general run of un-professional buyers. They invariably raise difficulties the moment the subject of copyright is mentioned, insomuch that a young painter, who dare not jeopardise a sale, pre-fers to let drop the copyright altogether and trust to no harm coming of it, while the man of eminence in his pro-fession sells to dealers who will sign (Form 1), and the purchaser buys the picture without the copyright from the dealer at an enhanced price.*

B. : I understand very little about the question, I admit ; but I cannot get rid of the idea that you are withholding something.

A. : I am withholding nothing, as I hope presently to convince you. Look at that picture ; the forms I use are old enough and universal enough, in all conscience. Then I take certain colours ; those colours are colours open to all. It is the particular grouping of the forms and the particular arrangement of the colours which create the individuality of that picture, and distinguish it from all other pictures. In other words, the design is a property which the law says is mine, that property being the right to prevent the public from depriving me of the profits I may derive from the exclusive reproduction of my work.

B. : But how can you separate this property from the picture? It must go with it.

A. : Not so. The notion that nothing is property which cannot be ear-marked and recovered in detinue or trover may be true in an early stage of society, when pro-perty is in its simple form, and the remedies for violation of it also simple; but it is not true in a more civilised state, when the relations of life, and interests arising therefrom become complicated. In other matters the law has been adapted to the progress of society, according to justice and

* Evidence of Basil Field, Esq., before Copyright Commission, 1878.

convenience, and by analogy it should be the same with artistic works ; and they would become property, with all its incidents, on the most elementary principles of securing to industry its fruits and to capital its profits.   It is just, not only to the artist, but useful to the community.*

B. : Well, I admit the existence of two properties, but I say that, having bought the one, I ought to have the other.

A. : My contention is that, having created the two properties, which the law recognises as distinct, I ought not to be deprived of one because I sell the other.   I cannot compel you to sign my form, except by declining to sell, but I think you are morally bound to do so. In reality, my retention of copyright is a protection to you.

B. : In what way ?

A. : I have here the original oil sketch which I made for the picture you wish to buy, and for which I have been offered £100.   I have also, as you see, upon my easel a highly finished study of the same design in water colour. If no agreement is made between us, the purchasers of these will be able to reproduce them in any form they please. It is, therefore, to your interest, as well as to mine, that a definite arrangement should exist.

B. : Very well ; I ask you to sign an agreement to give me the copyright (Form 2†).

A. : Then in that case I shall be obliged to charge a higher price for the sacrifice, for I shall be obliged to destroy my original sketch and the water colour study, although they were both absolutely necessary to me in order to enable me to complete the painting of your picture.

B. : But the value of my picture would be increased, would it not, by the exhibition of your water colour study, and by the sale of your original sketch ?

A. : Undoubtedly. In a sale at Christie's I have known Mr. Woods say, " The study for this work was sold in

* Sir Wm. Ele, in Jefferys v. Boosey, 4 H. L. C. 867.
† See Appendix.

this room for £—," in order to enhance the value of the more important work. But you will not get this advantage unless you give me the copyright in the original picture. What is good for me and good for you, will, unless you comply with my request, lead to evil for us both.

B.: I don't understand.

A.: If I have the copyright, I can sell these original sketches, and also other small studies which I have made for the picture, without the right of reproduction. But if no agreement is made between us, the owner of the original sketch in oil, or of the water colour study, or of any of those small studies, will be able to reproduce his purchase, as I pointed out before, in any way in which he likes.

B.: Then we come back to the same point. I would again suggest that you should assign the copyright to me.

A.: Then I must ask you to buy all three pictures and the copyright of the original.

B.: But I don't want three pictures of the same class.

A.: Just now you said you did not want half a picture; but there is no alternative. The only way out of the difficulty is to let me reserve the copyright.

B.: But without any agreement being signed I could surely keep the picture and publish engravings of it myself?

A.: Certainly. But you might want to sell the picture or to publish it; in which case some one else could at once publish a similar engraving, or cheap and bad copies, thus injuring the sale and value of your property. Besides, there will be the study and the original sketch unprotected.

B.: But I complain of the latter; you have no right to sell those.

A.: I was obliged to make the study of the design, and the original sketch; they cost me both more time and more actual brain-work, in order to complete them, than your picture. Am I to be deprived of all reward for this work, which was rendered necessary in order to create what you buy? You must either pay for this work, or your complaints are wholly without foundation. In selling them to others I relieve you from paying me the sum which I realise by their sale. The exhibition of them enhances the value of your property, yet you refuse to give me the copyright in the latter, although one effect of your so doing would be to protect your engravings should you wish to issue them.

B. : Assuming that you have the copyright, what is to protect me from further replicas by you ?

A. : I am not at all likely to make any ; my reputation would suffer, like the reputation of the few artists of eminence who have done such things. This, however, is a pure matter of business ; so, putting all question of honour and moral duty aside, I would give you an undertaking concurrently with your signing (Form 1), binding myself not to issue a replica of the same size, material, or scheme of colour.

B. : Well, to return to the engraving of which we were speaking. I should have a separate copyright in that, should I not ? and if so, the issue of a second engraving would be an infringement of that copyright.

A. : You would have a copyright in your engraving *provided that the name of the proprietor and the date of the first publication were truly engraved on each plate, and were printed on every impression ;** but if you parted with your picture, or published it, you could . not prevent any person from going to the original picture and making therefrom a similar engraving, so long as he did not make use of any of the work on your plate. Practically, however, the only pirate of an engraving is the photographer, owing to the difficulty there is in proving any other copy to be mechanically exact.

B. : But why should I not register the copyright in this painting directly I have it delivered to me ?

A. : You could register the copyright, it is true ; but so could I, for that matter, or, in fact, any one else, for they make no enquiries at Stationers' Hall. You fill up and

* 8 Geo. II., c. 13 ; and 7 Geo. III., c. 38.

sign a form,* pay your shilling, and the thing is done; but registration does not give you anything which you have not already.† Besides, there is a penalty for making a false entry in the book.

B.: But the entry is *prima facie* evidence of ownership of the copyright.‡ I could bring an action and give the entry in evidence.

A.: Yes, and the first question that would be asked of you in cross-examination would be, "Was there a written memorandum signed by the artist at the time you bought the picture?" Your answer in the negative, or mine to the same effect—for I should probably have to be there as a witness—would stop the case, for it would show that there was no copyright in existence, and never could be. Besides, look at the form of registration. You have to insert the date of the memorandum; and how could you fulfil that requirement? It is moreover a misdemeanour to make a false entry.§

B.: But I know of hundreds of paintings not painted on commission which have been registered without any document having been signed either by the buyer or the artist.

A.: It is done every day; but that proves nothing, except the amount of ignorance, or of something worse, that prevails on the subject of copyright. *Registration* without the *Right to Register* is of no avail if a case concerning the copyright of a picture crops up in a court of law.

B.: But tell me further what is the exact effect of registration.

A.: It enables the proprietor of the copyright in a painting to sue for piracy. He cannot sue until registration, nor then for anything done prior to registration.

B.: If it is a condition precedent to the right to stop

* See Appendix.
† Lucas v. Cooke, L.R. xiii., Ch. Div. 873.
‡ 5 and 6 Vict., c. 45, s. 11.
§ Fine Arts Act, 1862; 5 and 6 Vict., c. 45, s. 12. For Form, see Appendix.

piracy, one would imagine that the entries of original proprietorship of paintings are very numerous at Stationers'
Hall.

A.: No, that is not the case; the artists are very negli-
gent in that respect.*

B.: Suppose, for instance, that piratical copies have
been made of an unregistered picture, and I am the innocent purchaser of them, and that you are the owner of the
copyright?

A.: In that case, the moment I register I can give you
notice not to part with your copies for the purposes of
sale, hire, exhibition, or distribution, and enforce penalties
in case you disregard my notice.

B.: Then ignorance in no excuse for me?

A.: That is so under the Engraving Acts.   In 17 Geo.
III., c. 57, the words "knowing the same to be printed or
reprinted," which occur in 8 Geo. II., c. 13, being left
out; but in certain cases under the Fine Arts Act guilty
knowledge has to be proved.

B.: Could you not go against the real culprit, the original pirate, in the case just put to you?

A.: No, for his act took place prior to registration.
Such is the present state of the law.

B.: Must the original assignment of copyright and all
interim assignments be registered in cases where copyright has changed hands?

A.: No; it is sufficient that the assignment to the person registering be registered.   There must be a memorandum in writing (either Form 1 or Form 2) to begin
with, and all interim assignment must be in writing,
signed by the person assigning the copyright,† otherwise
the person registering will have no title.

B.: I don't exactly see the use of registration.

A.: It is simply a cheap and easy form of *primâ facie*
evidence of title, and convenient to art publishers,
whose works are very frequently pirated.   To all other

* Evidence of the Registrar before the Royal Commission.
† Fine Arts Act, s. 3.

persons it is an unmitigated evil, as being a condition precedent to right of action, which often, when neglected, protects the evil doer, and which gives the injured party, when complied with, no advantage that he would not have were registration unnecessary.

B. : Now, supposing I sign this document (Form 1), what use do you intend to make of the copyright?

A. : I wish for the future to protect myself from bad copies and spurious imitations of my work, the circulation of which will also affect you, by casting doubt upon and depreciating the value of my genuine work. When I find my paintings reproduced in inferior chromo-lithography, badly engraved, reproduced in colours often different to those in the original, it is high time for me to look after my reputation. It was only the other day that a subject of my picture, representing a child in mourning, was reproduced with the child in a flaming scarlet frock, taking all the point and sentiment out of the design. I have also known dealers who have engraved the picture, and then have produced the engraving in two halves, creating a subject that was never in the artist's mind at all at the time he painted the original picture. Then, again, one does not want the designs of one's pictures hawked about on advertisements for patent mustard, and other articles, nor sent round in circulars and such like modes of advertisement.

B. : But surely you could trust me to protect your interests. Why not give me the copyright?

A. : I should be satisfied to do so were I certain that the picture and the copyright would both continue to be your property. You may, however, sell the picture, and in order to protect me you would have to undertake not to part with the copyright. At your death it would pass, without mention under your will, as part of your residuary personal estate, or go to your next-of-kin in case of your dying intestate. The owner (who might be the trustee of a marriage settlement!) would not in all probability know that he possessed it, so that any piracy of it would go on with impunity. On the other hand, had I the copyright,

c

I should be able to check an infringement at once. Besides, well-known artists, or their representatives, are always accessible to publishers or engravers, whereas in cases where a picture has changed hands it is often, for the reasons just given, impossible to know where the copyright is, or whether any exists.

B. : You would not object to a good mezzotinto engraving or etching, I presume?

A. : On the contrary, either the one or the other would do my reputation good.   I will, if you choose, sell you a license to copy (Form 5 *) my work in either of those ways, keeping the copyright in order to protect myself from bad reproduction of my picture by others ; but you are not an art publisher by trade, so you could not profitably engrave my picture.

B. : How so?

A. : You could not give the retail trader any guarantee as to the number of proofs taken from the plate, or as to the nature of the impression. He would therefore refuse to buy. In the case of a professional art publisher it is known by the position of an embossed stamp, marked on the margin of an engraving by the " Print Sellers' Association," whether a certain impression is *bond-fide* an " artist's proof "—" proof before letters " or " proof after letters," as the case may be ; and the Association will only stamp the number of proofs of each class declared by the publisher before publication.

B. : I do not want to engrave the picture; but assuming that I did, what guarantee should I have that you would not engrave the picture yourself? You would still have the right to engrave.

A. : Yes ; but not having the picture, I could not exercise such a right.   And if I gave you the license, I would append an undertaking not to reproduce in the same material and size, if you desired it (Form 5).

B. : Surely the possession of the copyright imports a power of access to the picture.

* See Appendix. Lucas v. Cooke, L.R. xiii, Ch. Div., 872.

A.: By no means; that is a popular error. You can hide your picture from the sight of man if you like. Until you publish the picture you can proceed against any person who copies it without your leave.* This right of yours is a common law right, and is quite distinct from the copyright which I wish to reserve. You could proceed against me if I used your picture to copy while it was in your possession, notwithstanding that I had the copyright. We could both of us proceed against the third party above mentioned—you at common law for damages for copying your property without your leave,† and I for damages and penalties under the Fine Arts Act, 1862, for infringing my copyright.

B.: What amounts to a piracy within the meaning of the Fine Arts Act, 1862?

A. : Under that statute a picture may not be reproduced or colourably imitated in any material or by any process. It is, therefore, an offence to imitate a picture by statuary or photography.

B. : Would a photograph of an engraving of a picture be an infringement of the copyright in a picture?

A.: Yes; when the subject of a picture is copied it is of no consequence whether that is done directly from the picture itself, or through intervening copies. If in the result that which is copied be an imitation of the picture, then it is immaterial whether that be arrived at either by direct or intermediate steps.‡

B.: But suppose I bought a license to engrave your picture; surely I might photograph the engraving and sell that?

A. : Certainly not; that would be an infringement of my copyright in the picture.

B. : But you told me that I should also have copyright in the engraving.

A.: That is perfectly true, but the protection given by

---

* Prince Albert v. Strange, 18. L.J. Ch., 120.   1 Mac and Gor, 25.
† *Ib.*
‡ *Exparte* Beal, 3 L.R.Q.B., 387.

the Engraving Acts is only commensurate with the skill of the engraver. What right has he to the reproduction of the design? That is my work, and is consequently protected by the copyright in my picture.

B.: Then what is the use of the copyright in the engraving if the law is as you state?

A.: To give the engraver protection for his own meritorious work. Look at this beautiful print, "The Huguenot," engraved by Oldham Barlow from Mr. Millais' picture. It is difficult to conceive any skill or art much higher than that which has, by a wonderful combination of lines and touches, reproduced the very texture and softness of the hair, the very texture and softness of the dress, and the expression of love and admiration in the eyes of the lady looking up at her lover. That art or skill was the thing which, as I believe, was intended to be protected by the Engraving Acts.*

B.: But suppose the engraver or etcher was also the designer?

A.: Then part of his meritorious work would be the design, which would also be protected. The first Engraving Act (8 Geo. II., c. 13) only gave protection to the engraver who was also the designer of his work, owing, I suppose, to the fact that Hogarth,† who caused the Act to be introduced, was generally the designer of his engravings.

B.: You said just now that I could acquire copyright in an engraving provided that the name of the proprietor, and the date of first publication, were truly engraved on each plate, and printed on every print: would the issue of one copy without such words being printed thereon vitiate the copyright?

A.: It would.

B.: I always see "Published by so-and-so," and have

---

* Dicks v. Brooks, L.R. xv., Ch. Div., 22.

† On this statute being passed Hogarth designed and engraved a small plate in commemoration of the event. An inscription on the print says that the Act was "obtained by the endeavours, and almost at the sole expense, of the designer of this print, in the year 1735."

always thought it was the publisher's name that ought to be engraved on the print, not the proprietor's.

A. : Many publishers think so, and will tell you they are right ; but the Act says "proprietor."* Therefore, if the publisher is not also the proprietor, there is no copyright; because the proprietor's name is not on the print.†

B. : With regard to the date—why is that to be placed on the plate ?

A. : In order to enable a person to know when the engraving was first published, and whether the copyright has expired or not. Accuracy with regard to the date is essential.‡

B. : Has the copyright in an engraving, print, etching, or lithograph to be registered ?

A. : No; registration has nothing whatever to do with copyright, in these subjects, but notwithstanding this, many publishers are stupid enough to go to Stationers' Hall and register their engravings, or the copyright in the original picture when they do not possess it. It is a loss of the fee, and a trouble for nothing.

B. : Let us return to our subject, my picture. It seems to me that neither I nor my family could copy my picture for amusement or study, if the copyright remained with you.

A. : The penal clauses of the Act are limited to copying for " sale, hire, exhibition, or distribution ; " so that your picture would be available for the purposes you name.§

B. : Notwithstanding that I am not prepared to buy a license to engrave, I should very much like to possess a good engraving of the picture.

A. : Give me the copyright in my work, and you may at no distant date be able to possess such an engraving. It generally happens in this way—A publisher, on learning from me, the artist, that I have the copyright, will ask who

* See Appendix.
† Thompson v. Symonds, 5 T.R., 41.
‡ Bonner v. Field; see Thompson v. Symonds, 5 T.R., 44.
§ Fine Arts Act, 62, s. 6; Appendix.

has the picture.   He will then go to you and say, " If you
will let me have the picture for engraving—I have leave
from the artist—I will employ a first-rate engraver, and it
will be thoroughly well done under the supervision of the
artist, and the proofs touched by him.   I will give you so
much, or so many proofs, for the loan of the picture, and
engage not to keep it more than a certain time."   The
result is that you, the purchaser, get the immense advantage of having the picture well engraved, because a well
engraved work is worth very much more in the market. I,
the artist, get the advantage of having my work well engraved, which is a capital advertisement, and also a sum
of money from the publisher, both for the license to
engrave (Form 5 *) and for correcting or touching the
proofs.   The publisher gets the advantage of having a
good title.   The public get a good engraving instead of
a bad one, and the artist-engraver is employed instead
of some of the herd of cheap-jacks who are employed
when no title can be made.†

B. : I will sign your document with pleasure. (Form 1.)

A. : Thank you.   You may rely on me that any license
given by me to reproduce your picture will have no
other effect than to enhance the value of it ; but you
will have the right of veto, if you choose, upon any
scheme for reproduction, because, as pointed out above,
no one can gain access to it while it remains in your
possession.   The copyright you have given me lasts, remember, for my lifetime, and for seven years from the
date of my death.

B. : That seems a very short and uncertain time.

A. : Yes, especially as an artist's reputation and popu-
larity are usually of slow growth.   Besides, it often takes
three or four years to engrave a picture, so that a copyright
is of very little value to the artist's widow.   In any
future legislation there is little doubt that the term will
be for the life of the artist, and for thirty years after his
death.

* See Appendix.
† Evidence of Basil Field, Esq., before Copyright Commission.

B. : What are the chief forms of piracy now-a-days?

A. : To begin with, I suffer much from imported works. Lithographs are made abroad—generally in Germany—from prints which have been published over here from my pictures. These lithographs are then imported into this country, and hawked about, or sold by the inferior print-sellers, at an exceedingly cheap rate. Vulgar and distorted things they are, too, as a rule.

B. : Then the proprietor of the engraving suffers as much as you do?

A. : Yes.

B. : But is there no remedy?

A. : There is the 10th section of the Fine Arts Act,* which absolutely prohibits the importation, and gives power to the Custom House Officers to detain any copies declared by the owner of the copyright to be piratical; but the rubbish gets smuggled in, and then the difficulty is to prove guilty knowledge in the party selling, so that prosecutions hardly ever occur.

B. : But is this traffic in piratical copies very great?

A. : It is; it extends all over the country.

B. : It seems to me that all you want is a systematic and vigorous prosecution of offenders. The law might certainly be amended in one instance—viz., by giving a power of immediate seizure; but apart from that, the remedies provided appear to me adequate to put a stop to these practices. A society, employing paid detectives to be always on the watch, would have a deterrent effect, I should think. Do you suffer in any other way?

A. : Yes; photographs are made in this country from engravings of my works, which are hawked about from door to door. Before they can be seized the hawker must be summoned, and he generally vanishes before a summons can be served.

B. : In this case also the publisher of the engraving suffers; but how does this affect you? A photograph is generally an exact, and not a distorted copy of your work; it cannot injure your reputation.

* See Appendix.

A.: If the publisher of the engraving cannot secure his monopoly, he consequently cannot give me the price for the picture, or for the right to engrave, which he otherwise would do.   As a matter of fact, these prices have fallen immensely since this form of piracy has been prevalent; publishers will not pay what they used to do.

B.: You want the law remedied by the giving of an immediate power of seizure in this case, as well as in the case of imported piracies.

A.: Yes; an immediate power of seizure at the risk of the person who authorised the seizure, if he subsequently failed to prove the ownership of copyright in himself.

B.: Would you allow such power of seizure in case the hawker had bought innocently?

A.: Yes; leaving it to the discretion of the magistrate to remit the penalty in such a case—if he thought fit to do so.

B.: Is there any other form of piracy?

A.: Yes.   The making copies of pictures, signing them, and selling them as originals.

B.: But that is forgery, surely.

A.: No, not at Common Law;* but the 7th section of the Fine Arts Act† meets the case.   You could not have better legislation on the subject, but it is difficult to carry out the law in practice.   I have half-a-dozen such copies of my works submitted to me every year.

B.: But have you no right to detain or to destroy such copies?

A.: No.   I must first prove that the person submitting the copy to me is privy to the fraud.   But I could give him notice not to part with it for sale, hire, exhibition, or distribution, if I possessed the copyright in the original.

B.: Of course you could not interfere with mere imitation of your style unless your signature be also forged, and then the case would come under the 7th section.

A.: That is so, and I hope soon that we shall have an

* See p. 5.   †† See Appendix.

Act* passed which will give a power to search houses for piratical copies and photographs of pictures, the only way in which this, and the other forms of piracy can be stopped.

B.: Can the owner of the copyright in a painting alter the painting?

A.: No, except by the artist's consent. Look at section 7, sub-sec. 4, of the Fine Arts Act, it runs thus with regard to paintings—"Where the author or maker of any painting made either before or after the passing of this Act shall have sold or otherwise parted with the possession of such work, if any alteration shall afterwards be made therein by any other person, by addition or otherwise, no person shall be at liberty, during the life of the author or maker of such work, without his consent to make or knowingly to sell or publish, or offer for sale, such work or any copies of such work so altered as aforesaid, or of any part thereof, as or for the unaltered work of such author or maker." This section says "No person," so that the owner of copyright is barred by it.

B.: That seems a very fair provision for the protection of the artist.

A.: Yes; but it does not go far enough, as I will presently show you. Mr. Charles Landseer painted a picture entitled "The Eve of the Battle of Edgehill," which contained, amongst other things, two dogs, which had been wrought upon by his brother, Sir Edwin Landseer, and greatly improved. A dealer, who bought the picture, cut out the dogs and sold them as Sir Edwin's work, and, filling up the hole in the original painting with two dogs painted by a third and third-rate artist, sold it as the work of Charles Landseer.

B.: Such a case is within the plain words of the section.

A.: Yes, for the framers of the Act had it before them

* See Appendix, for the Law Amendment Society's Report on Copyright and for the Copyright Bill of 1881.

when they presented the Bill. But listen to this. A dealer buys my picture and the copyright. It represents an animal and three figures, and has a title indicative of the idea which I wish to convey. The picture is engraved in its entirety by a well-known engraver, and the engravings are published; but subsequently the design is cut in half, the animal and one figure only appearing, under a different title and with the announcement that the work is by me, although the idea conveyed by the mutilated design is one which I never had in my mind at all at the time I painted the original picture.

B.: Surely this comes within the spirit of the 4th subsection.

A.: It is doubtful whether it comes within the letter of it, which seems to point to an alteration in the original picture; but that section could be very easily altered to meet the case by the insertion of "or in the design of" after "therein," and by the insertion of "such work or any copies of such work or of the design thereof so altered as aforesaid" after "offer for sale." *

.

* See Appendix.

CHAPTER III.

COMMISSIONED WORK.

DIALOGUE.

[Enter (C.) a gentleman who has commissioned A. to paint him a picture.]

C.: So you have finished my commission; does the copyright belong to me?

A.: It does, as nothing was agreed about it at the time you desired me to paint the picture.

C.: But I thought some agreement in writing was necessary under the Fine Arts Act, 1862, in all cases where a painting, drawing, or the negative of a photograph, is first sold.

A.: In all cases except where the work has been commissioned as in this case.*

C.: How do you define work done on commission?

A.: If you ask me to paint you a picture for a valuable consideration, and I paint it, that is a commission, whether the subject is suggested by you or not.

C.: I like that sketch on your easel. Suppose I ask you to paint that, would it be commissioned work?

A.: The prevailing opinion is that it would; but on the other hand it must be remembered that copyright is only given to an "original" work. When my abstract conception has been already expressed in a sufficiently concrete form, as in that sketch, for you to judge whether you would like it or not; the design exists, and it is doubtful whether a more complete artistic representation of it would be held to be an " original " work to which copyright would attach.

* See Appendix.

C.: Why should there be any difference as regards copyright between a picture that has been commissioned and one that has been simply painted and offered afterwards for sale?

A.: Again you put to me a poser. It is the artist's work in each case, and it can hardly be said that the man who merely suggests a subject is entitled to a valuable property in the work when produced. If he actually made the design the case would be altered. My opinion is that the law should give all copyright to the artist in the absence of agreement; but I would have a reservation forbidding him to use his right of reproduction, in the case of portraits taken on commission, without the consent of the person commissioning the work, and perhaps a similar provision against the issuing of replicas without consent.

C.: I understand that you make these exceptions rather on the ground of deference to public opinion than in deference to the wish of artists.

A.: In deference to public opinion, to which the artists have no objection, and to get over certain difficulties with regard to portraiture and replicas. The Copyright Commissioners recommend that, in future, copyright in paintings and drawings should vest in the purchaser, in the absence of agreement, instead of falling to the ground, as it does now in all cases where work is not commissioned. On the other hand, the artists say that it should vest in them, and that the recommendation of the Commissioners is an unjust one as far as they are concerned. The Commissioners reply that the difficulties above-mentioned prevent their giving copyright to the artist. But in their report the Commissioners, in dealing with photographs which they propose to class (as they ought to be classed if classed at all with other works of art) with engravings rather than with paintings, make a provision with regard to portraits taken by photography, and say that the copyright of these should be in the photographer, without the power of reproduction in the absence of the consent of the person commissioning the work. The artists are willing to agree to a similar reservation in the case of portraits and replicas, and this being the case, it certainly seems unjust to them that they should not be able to retain their property without formal agreement.

C.: It seems to me that your proposal is the fairer one of the two, for it gets over the one point on which the artists ought to give way. There is no doubt that a man who gives a commission for a portrait of his wife, or daughter, or himself, should have the absolute and entire control of the copyright, as a veto on any sort of republication ; but would you not have a difficulty in defining a portrait?

A.: Practically none whatever.

C.: Would the word include the portrait of an animal—of a dog, for instance?—and if so, would it include a pack of hounds, or a picture of a house or a room, or any object without life? Is it to include pictures of persons taken in character, not so much for the sake of the portrait of the person as for the sake of groups where the scene is the object of the work, though the pictures of the persons present are portraits?

B.: These difficulties are rather apparent than real. But the objection will apply equally to the reservation of the Commissioners in the case of photographic portraits mentioned just now.

C.: I feel another difficulty. Suppose I were to ask Mr. Stacey Marks, R.A., to execute some of his beautiful decorative designs in my house?

A.: That being commissioned work, you would, under the law as it stands, have the copyright.

C.: But under the future law, as advocated by you, it would vest in him. I should not like him to repeat my decorations elsewhere.

A.: He would be very unlikely to do so, for the sake of his own reputation, if for no other reason ; but the real question is which of the two should have the trouble of insisting on an agreement. It is his design, but under the law at present the copyright goes to you unless you sign an agreement.   I say that it should go to him unless he agrees with you that it should not do so.   You would have no difficulty in obtaining from him an undertaking not to reproduce the design.   Besides, it is only fair that he should have the copyright, in order to protect himself and the owner of the house from bad copies of the design.

C. : How do you mean ?

A.: Under the present law the copyright as before pointed out is in you. In case you part with the house, and forget—as you no doubt would forget—to assign the copyright in writing to the future lessee or to your landlord, the copyright would remain with you, and neither the future owner nor Mr. Marks could sue a pirate, who, perhaps, might have taken the house simply for the purpose of piracy. There was a case which came under my notice where, without any written agreement, an associate of thè Royal Academy was employed to make some decorative designs for a theatre. That was done on commission, and the designs were exceedingly popular. The person giving the commission got into difficulties, and sold the theatre. The present owners of the theatre, and, therefore, of the decorations, and the artist who designed them, cannot between them prevent pirates from making copies, and generally very bad copies, of them.

C. : Well, to return to the picture you have painted for me. Supposing it had been agreed that you should reserve the copyright, would any memorandum be necessary in that case ?

A. : Yes.   I should then have asked you to be good enough to sign this document (Form 1), which would vest the copyright in me.   I invariably make the purchaser of my pictures, whether done on commission or otherwise, sign this document, except in a case where I paint a portrait, for then I feel that the copyright, or rather the veto on repetition, should go with the picture. A good etching or engraving of those pretty faces would do my reputation good, and considering that the subject is a group of your daughters, and that you are a man of position, it is extremely unlikely that you will allow any bad copies of my work to be produced.

C.: Was there a binding contract between us as to this picture?

A.: There must be either a written memorandum of the commission signed by the person to be charged with the contract, or the purchaser must give something in earnest to bind the bargain or in part payment; otherwise I should not be bound to execute the picture, nor you to accept and pay for it when executed. You will, remember, however, that I asked you for a small cheque on account, which you gave me, so that there was a binding contract between us.*

C.: But I suppose you could have kept me waiting an unconscionable time for my picture?

A.: I should have been bound to deliver your portrait within a reasonable time, as time was not mentioned.

C.: Of what use is the copyright to me?

A.: You hold the picture free from any interference on the part of any one. Register your copyright at Stationers' Hall (which you may do for 1s.) at once; you then can sue for any reproduction of it which may take place after registration in my life-time and until seven years after my death. You need never trouble your head as to whether you have by any act published your picture; you can sell the picture or give it away without feeling any anxiety that bad copies of it may be produced with impunity.

C.: You have, I notice, some studies and sketches made for my picture. Would the sale of these amount to an infringement of my copyright?

A.: Technically I should be inclined to say it would; but various opinions have been given on the subject. Before I can paint my pictures I frequently find it necessary to make a number of sketches or studies, which, grouped together, make up the picture in its finished state. These works may be studies expressly made for

* "Statute of Frauds," see Chap. XI.

the picture about to be painted, or they may be sketches which have been made at various times and kept as materials for future pictures. If the law is as I am in-clined to think, it is certainly a great hardship to me that I should not be allowed to sell them.

C. : I should doubt whether your fears would prove well grounded if a case was ever brought into court. My copyright could not be injured by their sale. They are re-produced in my picture, but in a more or less altered shape, and combined with other independent work. You would surely be safe as long as you did not reproduce the original design.

A. : I am inclined, on consideration, to come round to your view, although no less a person than the late Lord Westbury thought otherwise. Of course, if the copyright remained with me, I should be protected, but as it is now yours, perhaps you would be good enough to sign a memor-andum giving me liberty to sell the studies and sketches (Form 4*), so that I should be safe in case you assigned your copyright to some other person.

C. : If I sell my picture without mentioning the copy-right, does it lapse ?

A. : No ; it remains with you, as pointed out just now with regard to the house decoration, and you could sell it to me if you chose.   I have frequently bought up some of my old copyrights cheap from dealers who have parted with the pictures, and I have stopped a great deal of bad reproduction by that means.

[Enter (E.) the Editor of an Art Periodical.]

E. : I want a subject of yours for my Christmas number.

A. : I have nothing ready but those two pictures which you see there.   One has been painted on commission for Mr. Agnew ; the other is at your service.

E. : I like them both, but prefer Mr. Agnew's.

* See Appendix.

A. : The copyright is in him.

E. : Then I should have, I suppose, to purchase the copyright from Mr. Agnew in order to publish a wood engraving in my journal ?

A. : No ; all you want is a license (Form 5*) from Mr. Agnew. I have nothing to do with the case. If I allowed you to copy the picture he could proceed against us both—against me for breach of trust, and against you for infringement of his right. You must go to him, and I have no doubt he will grant you what you require.

E. : I think, perhaps, I should be delayed if I went to him, and so must be content with your second picture.

A. : Give me what I ask for the picture, and I will give you a license to engrave it on wood (Form 5). You must, however, sign this document (Form 1), in order to vest the copyright in me. In my license to you I will undertake not to produce a wood engraving of your picture; and you will then, having the picture in your possession, possess the right of veto on any scheme for reproduction by me. Thus I shall be able to protect my reputation, while you will be able to protect your property.

E. : But have I any copyright in my wood-cut when engraved ?

A. : How do you intend to bring it out ?

E. : In my periodical, combined with letterpress.

A. : Has the first number of your periodical been registered under the Literary Copyright Act of 1842 ?

E. : No.

A. : Then you have started a difficult point ; but I think you have copyright in your wood-cut, in the same way that you would have copyright in an engraving—*i.e.*, to the extent that no one could make use of your meritorious work. You could, however, make yourself perfectly safe by having your name cut in the block, with the date of publication, and printed on every print.†

* As to effect of license, see p. 18.

† See Cox v. Land and Water Company L.R. 9, Eq., 324 ; Bogue v. Houlston, *post*, p. 45.

E. : But if I had no copyright what is to protect you?

A. : Any copy of your wood-cut is an infringement of my copyright in the picture; so I am perfectly safe.

E. : I could sue in your name, if you gave your consent and if I indemnified you against the costs, I suppose?

A. : Yes.

E. : Do your ever make designs for Christmas cards or for valentines?

A. : I have a few sketches which might do for the purposes you mention.   How do you propose to bring them out?

E. : By chromo-lithography and other processes.   How am I to protect myself with regard to them?

A. : It depends upon the process employed.   If you intend to use lithography they come under the Engraving Acts; if photography, or hand-painting, under the Fine Arts Act, 1862.

CHAPTER IV.

DIALOGUE ON PHOTOGRAPHY.

SCENE.—*Photographic Studio.—Enter a gentleman* (M.).

M.: I see that you have my portrait in your window labelled " Copyright."

PHOTOGRAPHER: May I ask your name?

M.: Lord H—

P.: Certainly, I have your portrait exhibited for sale both singly, and in a group combined with the portraits of your fellow Cabinet Ministers. Have you any objection?

M.: I wish, rather, to ascertain whether I have any right to object. What is the law in relation to photographic copyright?

P.: The law places photographs on a par with paintings and drawings; but curious difficulties arise in interpreting and applying the law, owing to the inherent difference which exists between the two. I should have thought that photographs, if they are to be classed for legislation at all with works of art, should have been dealt with by the Engraving Acts, since the processes of reproduction or printing off from the negative in the one case, and from the plate in the other, are somewhat nearly allied ; and, were it not that the Fine Arts Act, 1862, assumes that until that time there was no copyright in a photograph, it seems to me unquestionable that the words of an Act of Parliament* which gave copyright to lithographs, are wide enough to embrace photography also.

M.: I understand, then, that whenever paintings and drawings are mentioned in the previous dialogues the conversation would equally apply to photographs?

* 15 and 16 Vic., c. 12, s. 14.

P. : That is so.   But you must regard the negative of the photograph, and not the photograph itself, as that which corresponds to the painting.   Look, if you please, to this copy of the first section of the Fine Arts Act, 1862.* "The author of every original photograph shall have the sole and exclusive right of copying, engraving, reproducing, and multiplying such photograph, and the negative thereof by any means and of any size, for the term of the natural life of such author, and seven years after his death."

M. : Then the copyright to start with is in the photographer—

P. : Yes; but the effect of the rest of the section which follows is, that, upon the first sale of the negative, the copyright must be preserved by an agreement in writing, signed either by the vendor or purchaser of the negative, giving the copyright to the other party, otherwise it is irredeemably lost; except in cases where the negative is made on behalf of any other person for a good or valuable consideration, in which case the copyright, if no agreement is made, vests in the sitter or commissioner.

M. : Then, applying this to my photograph—the single one I mean—where is the copyright?   I paid you nothing, for you requested me to sit; and, if I remember rightly, you presented me with several copies from the negative.

P. : The work was not made for a good and valuable consideration, and there was no agreement.   The copyright accordingly vests in the author, and belongs to me.

M. : Do you mean to say that I could not, if I objected, prevent you from exhibiting my portrait for sale or otherwise—from hawking it about the streets, for instance?

P. : You could not stop me doing any of these things; you would be taken to have known why I wanted your portrait, for you came into my studio with your eyes open.

M.: Could I compel you to sell a copy to me?

P. : Certainly not, unless I had a copy exhibited for

* See Appendix.

sale in my window, for that would amount to an invitation to buy.

M. : But suppose I sold one of my portraits, which you gave me at the time, to the editor of a periodical, and he reproduced it by photography, or engraving, would that be an infringement of your copyright ?

P : It would.

M. : If the copyright was mine, I suppose I could prevent you from selling my portrait or exhibiting it in your window ?

P. : Yes ; and upon conviction before a magistrate, the negative would be forfeited by you.*

M. : But you have sold my photograph already, and have no agreement in writing reserving the copyright, therefore the copyright is lost, is it not ?

P. : No, the section† states " Upon the first sale of the *negative.*"   Although copyright is given by the first part of the section, to the photograph and the negative, the proviso for reservation, in case of a sale, deals only with the negative.   The negative of the photograph, as pointed out before, is thus placed on the same footing as a painting, in case of assignment or sale ; and in the forms,‡ " photograph and the negative thereof" should be substituted for " painting."

M. : What is an " original photograph ? "   I cannot understand my portrait being an " original " portrait, at least not in the sense in which the word " original " is applied to a painting.

P. : It is difficult to say what can be meant by an original photograph ; all photographs are copies of some object.   But a photograph taken from a picture, with consent of the owner is an original photograph, in so far that to copy it is an infringement of the statute.§

M. : But could you prevent me from sitting in the same attitude for another photographer ?

* Fine Arts Act, s. 6.
† Fine Arts Act, s. 1.
‡ See Appendix.
§ Graves Case, L.R. iv, Q.B. 723.

P. : No ; although it is unlawful to copy a photograph, or the negative, in which there is a subsisting copyright, it is permitted to copy the subject-matter of the photograph by taking another photograph.*

M. : Why do you put the word " copyright " on your photograph ?—is it required by the Act of Parliament ?

P. : It is not, and might just as well not be there.   It has been the custom of my firm to use the word, and this is all I know about it.

M. : Now with regard to the group.   You were commissioned to take that, by myself and colleagues, and were paid by us all as you supplied the copies.   Where is the copyright in the group ?

P. : It is clearly not in me ; and whether in all of you jointly, or jointly and severally, is a very difficult question. I think it rests with you all jointly ; but I fancy the question is one on which lawyers would wrangle until the Day of Judgment—in a Court of Law.

M. : If your view is correct, you would have required our joint signatures to a document reserving the copyright.

P. : Yes ; and you would now have to sue a pirate jointly.   This is one of the curious difficulties to which I just now alluded.

M. : Assume that you were to take one of the portraits out of the group, and were to issue it, without consent, could I proceed against you ?

P. : It would be clearly a piracy of the copyright in the group.†   According to my view you would have to proceed in the names of all the group, and to obtain their consent to the proceeding.   You would also have to have the names of all the group placed on the register, in order to enable you to proceed. (As to registration, see Dialogue, p. 15, *ante*.)

M. : Supposing that one member of the group had commissioned you to photograph it, and had paid for all the copies of the negative, would that alter the case ?

P. : It would.   The copyright would be in him alone.

* Fine Arts Act, 1862, s. 2.   † Fine Arts Act, ss. 6 and 11.

M.: Is there an individual copyright for each portrait, as distinct from the copyright in the group as a whole ?

P.: No ; but it may be created. For instance, you, with the consent of your group, might commission me to issue your portrait or the portrait of any other member of the group. The copyright of that portrait, when issued, would be in you ; or—

M.: Will removing or altering one portrait, alter or affect the nature of copyright in the group ?

P.: If done with the consent of the owner of the copyright, a new copyright is created in the alteration ; but if done without his consent it is an infringement, and cannot be the subject of copyright.

M.: Let me put this case to you —A negative is purchased by photographer A. from photographer B., who, forgetting whether it was done on commission or not, has previously registered the copyright ; does the copyright pass from B. to A. ?

P.: It cannot pass without a written agreement signed by B., as before pointed out; nor does it pass if B. had no title. Registration has nothing to do with the case as against the real owner.* If, therefore, the portrait was executed on commission, it remains in the sitter.

M.: Supposing the sitter hears of the infringement, against whom is he to go—against B. or his executors, or against A. ?

P.: He should go against all, or any, persons whom he finds pirating his property ; but he must remember that he must be registered in order to proceed at all, and that he cannot proceed then for anything done prior to registration.

M.: But A. is perfectly innocent in the matter.

P.: He may have his remedy against B. or his executors, for B. has sold without a title.

M.: Upon whom does the onus of proof of having paid for a negative lie ?

P.: It is impossible to give a general answer to your

* See Dialogue, p. 15 *ante.*

question, and I should have to be guided by the particular facts of any case which arose. Registration gives a *primâ facie* title to the proprietor as against all the world. So it would shift the onus of proof on to the person trying to contest the property of the person registered as proprietor.

M. : Supposing I consent to sit to you for one and a certain purpose—for instance, to appear in a certain picture, for which I do not pay—could you use my photograph for other purposes contrary to my wish ?

P. : No. Although I have a copyright in the negative of the portrait which you allow me to take, you have a right independent of the copyright laws altogether to prevent me from using your portrait, or my copyright, for any purpose other than that which was in my contemplation at the time I entered into the agreement.*

M. : Then in that case, if negatives, other than the one for which the sitting was given, were surreptitiously taken of me by you, you would be unable to publish such other photographs against my wish?

P. : That is so.

M. : Does the copyright in a portrait cease at the sitter's death ?

P. : The sitter's death has nothing to do with it. It ceases seven years after the death of the photographer, and devolves on the personal representatives of the proprietor, in the same way as any other personal property.

M. : Have such personal representatives of the owner of the copyright a right to claim the negative from the photographer ?

P. : They have only the right which the proprietor had. It is generally supposed that the copyright belongs to the commissioner, and the negative and the glass on which it is to the photographer.†

M. : Are your portraits much pirated ?

P. : Yes, to a great extent in illustrated newspapers and

---

* Prince Albert v. Strange, 2 De G. & Sm., 652.
† " Copinger on Copyright," 2nd Ed., p. 408.

other works. They are often reproduced in lithography abroad, especially in Hamburg, and imported into this country.

M. : Why do you not proceed against the pirates ?

P. : It has certainly occurred to us to do so, but when we have thought of the time and expense, we have not pursued the question.

M. : It seems to me, that if the law has provided you with remedies, and you do not take the trouble to avail yourselves of them, you have little right to complain. Surely, if the property is valuable, it would be worth while to give pirates an occasional wholesome lesson. Why not start a Photographers' Protection Society ? I suppose you have read the report of the Copyright Commission on the subject of photographs ?

P. : What is the substance of their recommendation as to any future legislation on the subject ?

M. : That copyright in photographs be for thirty years from publication, and copyright to belong to the proprietor of the negative ; but, in the case of photographs taken on commission, that no copies be sold or exhibited without the sanction of the person who ordered them.

P. : That seems a very fair and easy way of settling all, or nearly all, of the difficulties before alluded to, which exist under the present law in relation to photographs.

CHAPTER V.

COPYRIGHT IN ENGRAVINGS, ETCHINGS, AND LITHOGRAPHS, ETC.

THE copyright in engravings, &c., is created by the following statutes :—8 Geo. II., c. 13 ; 7 Geo. III., c. 38 ; 17 Geo. III., c. 57 ; which will be found in the Appendix. They are commonly known as the Hogarth Acts. 8 Geo. II., c. 13, was entitled—"An Act for the encouragement of the arts of designing, engraving, and etching historical and other prints, by vesting thé properties thereof in the inventors and engravers, during the time therein mentioned."

It recited that divers persons had, "by their genius, industry, pains, and expense, invented and engraved, or worked in mezzotinto, or chiaro-oscuro, sets of historical and other prints, in hopes to have reaped the sole benefit of their labours ; and that print-sellers and others had of late, without the consent of the inventors, designers, or proprietors of such prints, frequently taken the liberty of copying, engraving, and publishing, or causing to be copied, engraved, and published, base copies of such works, to the very great prejudice and detriment of the inventors, designers, and proprietors ; " and enacted that "every person who shall invent and design, engrave, etch, or work in mezzotinto or chiaro-oscuro, or from his own works and invention shall cause to be designed and engraved, etched, or worked in mezzotinto or chiaro-oscuro any historical or other print or prints, shall have the sole right and liberty of printing and reprinting the same for the term of 14 years, to commence from the day of the first publishing thereof, which shall be truly engraved with the name of the proprietor on each plate, and printed on every such print or prints." Spurious plates are to be forfeited to the proprietor of the original plate, and also the prints, together with 5s. for every print, to be recovered by any informer—half to the King and half to the informer.

By 7 Geo. III., c. 38, copyright is extended to work of which the engraver is not the designer. It enacts that prints of any portrait, conversation, landscape, or architecture, map, chart, or plan, or any other print or prints whatsoever, whether from the engraver's or etcher's own design,. or from any picture, drawing, model, or sculpture, whether ancient or modern, shall have the benefit of the former Act and of this Act. The same penalties are recoverable within six months of the offence, and the period of copyright is extended to 28 years from the first publication.

By 17 Geo. III., c. 57, a special action for damages is given to the proprietor; and 6 and 7 Wm. IV., c. 59, extends the three foregoing Acts to Ireland.

By 15 and 16 Vic., c. 12, s. 14, it was declared that the provisions of the four before-mentioned Acts are intended to include prints taken by lithography, or any other mechanical process, by which prints or impressions of drawings or designs are capable of being multiplied indefinitely, and the Acts shall be construed accordingly.

The following is an analysis of the provisions of the Hogarth Acts.* Every one has for 28 years from the first publishing thereof the sole right and liberty of multiplying, by any means whatever, copies of any print of whatever subject which he has.†

(1) Invented or designed, graved, etched, or worked in mezzotinto or chiaro-oscuro ; or which he has—

(2) From his own work, design, or invention, caused or procured to be designed, engraved, etched, or worked. in mezzotinto or chiaro-oscuro ; or which he has—

(3) Engraved, etched, or worked in mezzotinto or chiaro-

* Stephen's Dig. See Copyright Commissioners Report of 1878.
† Effect of 8 G. II., c. 13, s. 1, as enlarged and altered by 7 G. III., c. 38,. ss. 1, 2, 6. Extended to Ireland by 6 and 7 W. IV., c. 59, s. 1.

oscuro, or caused to be engraved, etched, or worked, from any picture, drawing, model, or sculpture, either ancient or modern.

Provided that such prints are truly engraved with the name of the proprietor, and the date of first publication on each plate, and printed on every print.

Prints taken by lithography and other mechanical pro-cesses are now upon the same footing as engravings.*

It will be seen that registration is not requisite for an engraving, etching, lithograph, or for any other work which comes under the Engraving Acts. Section 1 of 8 George II., c. 13,† requires " That the day of first publishing shall be truly engraved with the name of the proprietor on each plate, and printed on every such print or prints."

No action for infringement of copyright can be maintained unless these requirements are strictly carried out.

Many persons imagine that the *publisher's* name and not the proprietor's should be engraved. Unless the publisher is also the proprietor the error is fatal.

The designation " proprietor " need not be added to the name. In Graves v. Ashford,‡ L. C. B. Kelly said, " Upon the engraving before us we find these words— ' London : Published by Henry Graves & Co., May 1st, 1861, Printseller to the Queen, 6, Pall Mall.' Henry Graves and Co. are the proprietors of the engraving. The question is whether the legislature, when they required the name of the proprietor to appear, required that he should be expressly described as being the proprietor. They certainly have not said so in terms, and we must put a reasonable construction upon the words they have used. Every one who is at all conversant with these things looks at what is called the ' publication line ' for the name of the proprietor. The name which appears on the face of the print must be assumed to be that of the proprietor ; and it

---

* 15 and 16 Vic., cap. 12, s. 14.   Graves v. Ashford, L.R. 2 C.P. 410. Gambart v. Ball, 14 C.B.N.S. 306.   *Post*, p. 48.

† *Ante*, p. 42.

‡ L.R. 2 C.P. 421.

cannot alter the effect, or be less a compliance with the Act, because he is called the publisher. I think the statute has been substantially and literally complied with."

The trading name of the firm of proprietors is sufficient.* The exact date must appear.†

The only case where registration is necessary with regard to engravings, etchings, or lithographs, is where they form part of a book. In this case it is sufficient to acquire copyright in the book by registration under the Literary Copyright Act, 1842, and the works of art need not have the name of the proprietor and date of first publication engraved on the plate and printed on each print.

In the year 1851‡ Mr. Herrman Plonquet, of Stuttgard, contributed to the Great Exhibition in Hyde Park a number of stuffed animals, in single figures, and groups, in imitation of the actions of human beings. These figures having excited considerable attention and interest, Mr. David Bogue, bookseller and publisher, of Fleet Street, employed artists at great expense to make drawings from the figures and groups, and arranged a work consisting of letter press and wood cuts, representing these animals and groups of animals. This publication he sold at 3s. 6d. plain and 6s. coloured, under the title of " Comical Creatures from Wurtemburg, including the Story of Reynard the Fox, &c." The work, which consisted of a number of stories and fables, comprising the story of Reynard, an old tale in which no copyright existed, was published in the autumn of 1851, and soon reached a third edition. Mr. Bogue registered his property as a book. In January, 1852, Messrs. Houlston and Stoneman commenced the publication of a serial work entitled " The Story Book for Young People," and they issued the first number containing " The Comical History and Tragical End of Reynard the Fox," at the price of 2d. It appeared from the bill filed against them by Mr. Bogue, that his publication consisted of letter press-

* Rock v. Lazarus, L.R. 15, Eq. 104.
† Thompson v. Symonds, 5 T.R. 44.
‡ Bogue v. Houlston, 5 De G. and Sm: 267, 21 L.J.Ch: 70.

and woodcuts printed on the same large sheets of paper, and that the woodcuts appeared as separate leaves when the sheets were folded in their quarto size; it also appeared that the defendants were merely the publishers of the book for a Mr. Philp, who deposed that he had been engaged in designing and issuing various publications, in a cheap form, for the use and benefit of the poorer classes, and amongst them, illustrations of the Great Exhibition; that he had employed numerous artists to select objects for his work : that amongst the illustrations supplied to him were the sketches contained in the defendant's publication; and that the artist who supplied these sketches, by his affidavit, asserted that he had copied them from the original figures in the Exhibition. In granting an injunction against the defendants, Vice-Chancellor Parker, who was satisfied, upon inspection, that, although the stories were different, the designs of the defendants were copies of those of the plaintiff, for they had not only copied the designs, but the descriptive labels, said—"It has been suggested that the plaintiff has not made out any copyright in his designs, because he has not complied with the requisitions of the Act 8 Geo. II., c. 13, which regulates the copyright in engravings and designs, and which provides that the date of the publication, with the name of the proprietor of every engraving, should be engraved on each plate and printed on each print. But the plaintiff has acquired copyright in his book. It appears to me that a book must include every part of the book; it must include every print, design, or engraving which forms part of the book, as well as the letterpress therein, which is another part of it."

The foregoing case throws light on the question whether the proprietor of an unregistered illustrated newspaper has copyright in the woodcuts and engravings published therein. It has been decided in Cox v. *Land and Water* Journal Company* that the proprietor of a newspaper has, without registration, such a property in all its contents as will entitle him to sue in respect of a piracy, and applying

---

* L.R. 9, Eq.   See Bradbury v. Hotten, 42 L.J.Ex. 28.

the reasoning of Vice-Chancellor Parker in Bogue v. Houlston to this, it seems that if it is unnecessary to comply with the condition as to the proprietor's name and the date in the case of an engraving in a book, it can also be dispensed with in the case of a newspaper which has not been registered. The decision in Cox v. *Land and Water Company* is, however, a doubtful one.* Copyright, however, can be obtained by the proprietor of an illustrated journal, such as *Punch* or the *Illustrated London News*, by entering the title at Stationer's Hall, and complying with the requirements of s. 19 of the Literary Copyright Act, 1842.

ASSIGNMENT OF COPYRIGHT IN ENGRAVINGS, ETC.

Copyright in prints, engravings, and etchings can only be assigned by an agreement in writing, signed by the proprietor, and attested by two or more credible witnesses.†

For form of assignment of copyright in an engraving or etching see Appendix.‡

The purchaser of a plate can print without incurring penalties;§ but unless the copyright is assigned to him as well he cannot sue for piracy.

An assignee of the copyright is entitled to maintain an action for piracy under the Engraving Acts;‖ but it seems doubtful whether the name of the original proprietor of the plate or his assignee should be engraved thereon. The case of Bonner v. Field¶ seems to show that the name of the original proprietor should be left on the plate, with the date of first publication. To remove all doubt it would be well to engrave the name of the assignee as well.

* See note A to Art. 4 of Stephen's Digest. Appended to Report of Royal Commission, 1878.
† 17 Geo. III., c. 57. Kerr on Injunctions, 2nd Ed., p. 347.
‡ See Appendix.
§ 8 Geo. II., c. 13, s. 2.
‖ Thompson v. Symonds, 5 T.R. 41.
¶ *Ib.*, p. 44.

CHAPTER VI.

PIRACY OF ENGRAVINGS, ETCHINGS, AND LITHOGRAPHS.

A PIRATE under the Engraving Acts is a person who, without the consent of the proprietor in writing, signed by him and attested by two witnesses,*

(1) In any manner copies and sells, or causes or procures, to be copied and sold, in whole or in part, by varying, adding to, or diminishing from the main design, any copyright, print, &c.

(2) Prints, reprints, or imports for sale any such print, or causes or procures any such print to be so dealt with.

(3) Knowing the same to be so printed or reprinted, without the consent of the proprietor, publishes, sells, exposes for sale, or otherwise disposes of any such print or causes or procures it to be so dealt with.

The extent and nature of the protection afforded to the engraver and etcher under the Hogarth Acts is well illustrated by the two following cases, which show that the protection is of a twofold character :—

(1) The protection of the reputation of the engraver.

(2) The protection of the owner against any invasion of his commercial property in the print.

In the case of Gambart v. Ball,† C. J. Erle, in giving judgment in an action for the piracy of Rosa Bonheur's "Horse Fair" and Holman Hunt's "Light of the World," said :—"The question raised in this case is whether the publication and sale of photographic copies of engravings is an infringement of the rights given by the statutes of Geo. II. and Geo. III. I think it is. The code of statutes

---

* 8 Geo. II., c. 13, s. 1, as amended by 17 Geo. III., c. 57. See Appendix.
† 32 L.J.C.P., 166 ; 14 C.B.N.S. 306.

which protects rights of this kind begins with the 8 Geo. II., c. 13, and the preamble of that statute recites that print-sellers and others have, without the consent of the proprietors of engravings, published base copies of such engravings.   But the enacting part vests the property of all such prints in the inventor, and imposes a penalty on any person who shall engrave, etch, or copy as aforesaid, or in any other manner copy or sell any such print. That goes much beyond the recital of the statute, which might seem to point at an injury to the engraver by lowering the estimation of his work by publishing base copies of it.   It gives to the engraver a protection for the money value of that which is the product of his mind.   Then comes the 7 Geo. III., c. 38, which extends this protection to a longer period, and to a greater number of works, but the words which impose the restriction upon other persons copying such works are not so wide as those of the statute to which I am about to refer.   That is the 7 Geo. III., c. 57, which provides that if any person shall engrave, etch, or work in mezzotinto or chiaro-oscuro or otherwise, or in any other manner copy, in whole or in any part, any copies of prints and other matters therein mentioned, the party injured thereby shall have an action on the case against him.   That is the statute on which the present action is founded.   In the preamble it recites the two Acts to which I have already referred, and that they have been found ineffectual, and then goes on to use the extremely wide words which I have just read.   The question is whether the photographer who has taken photographic copies of a print is within the meaning of the Act.   The very statement of the question makes the answer self-evident.   The object of the statute was to secure to the inventor the commercial value of his article, as a reward for making an object of attraction, and as a stimulant to others to do likewise.   A photographic copy is as good, if not a better copy, than any other, whether it be on a large or a small scale.   It is not the extent of the paper, but the design placed upon it, and the ideas which.

E

that design conveys, that are the source of pleasure. Nor does it appear to me that it makes any difference that the copy is produced by a process not known at the time the statute was passed.   It is still a copy, and copying in any manner is prohibited by the statute.   It is clear that if these photographic copies were allowed to be made the commercial value of the print would be entirely destroyed. It was to protect the commercial value of these works of art that the statute was passed."

This judgment was upheld in the recent case of Dicks v. Brooks.*   The plaintiffs, who were the publishers and proprietors of a weekly periodical called " Bow Bells," had published, as an illustration for their Christmas number, 1877, a chromo-printed pattern for wool-work called the " Huguenot," being the copy of a design for Berlin wool, which had been imported by a German firm from Germany. The defendants—Messrs. Brooks and Sons, print-sellers and publishers, of the Strand—were the owners, by assignment, of the copyright in a print entitled the " Huguenot," engraved by Oldham Barlow from the original picture by Millais, the leading incident of which was the farewell of two lovers of different creeds on the eve of the massacre of St. Bartholomew. Upon the question whether the pattern for woolwork which was found to be taken from the defendants' print was a piracy of such print within the Hogarth Acts, Lord Justice James said :—" It appears to me that the Vice-Chancellor† fell into (if I may venture so to call it) the error of supposing that the case was within the Act 8 Geo. II., c. 13, which gave a protection not to a mere engraver, but to the man of genius, who, by his industry, pains, and expense, invented a design, ' or engraved, etched, or worked, or from his own work and invention caused to be designed and engraved, etched, or worked,' and so on, ' any historical print.'   The words were intended to give protection for the genius exhibited in the invention of the design, and the protection was commensurate with the in-

* L.R. xv., Ch. Div., 22.   † V. C. Bacon, in the Court below.

vention and design.   That Act was afterwards extended to
embrace the case of persons engraving from something
that was not the design of the engraver.   Now it appears
to me that the protection given by the subsequent Acts to
the mere engraver was intended to be, and was, commensurate with that which the engraver did, that the engraver
did not acquire against anybody in the world any right to
that which was the work of the original painter—did not
acquire any right to the design, did not acquire any right
to the grouping or composition, because that was not his
work, but the work of the original painter.   What, as it
seems to me, the Act gave him, and intended to give him,
was protection for his own meritorious work.   The art of
the engraver is often of the very highest character, and that
art or skill was the thing which, as I believe, was intended
to be protected by the Acts of Parliament; and what we
have to consider is whether the wool pattern before us (the
maker of which must have been aided in the production of
it by having before him the defendant's print, or some
kind of copy of it, because the wool pattern follows the
print in some particulars in which the print differs from
the picture) is a copy of the engraver's work.   It appears
to me, without going into any etymological definition of
the word 'copy,'* and using the word in the ordinary sense
of mankind as applied to the subject matter, the question
is, Is this a copy, is it a piracy, is it a piratical imitation
of the engraving, of that which was the engraver's meritorious work in the print?   Now, I am of opinion that
whatever may be the similarities between the one and the
other, the attempt not to reproduce the print, but to produce
something which has some distant resemblance to the print,
not by anything in the nature of the engraver's work, but
by what I may call a Mosaic of coloured parallelograms,
is not in any sense of the word a piratical imitation of the
print. Nobody would ever take it to be the print; nobody
would ever suppose that it was—to use the language of
the first Act—a base copy of the print.   It is a work of a

* As to what is a copy of a painting, see p. 68.

different class, intended for a different purpose, and, in my opinion, no more calculated to injure the print quâ print, or the reputation of the engraver, or the commercial value of the engraving in the hands of the proprietor, than if the same group were reproduced from the same engraving in waxwork at Madame Tussaud's, or in a plaster-of-Paris cast, or in a painting on porcelain."

The prints prohibited by the Engraving Acts are prints printed off from plates which are pirated from other engravings. Hence the sale of prints unlawfully struck off from the original plate does not amount to a piracy. Thus, where an engraver, being employed by the owner of certain drawings to engrave plates of those drawings, printed off from the plates, so engraved, a number of proofs, which he kept for himself, it was held that an action for piracy would not lay against him under the Engraving Acts, but that an action for breach of contract at common law was the proper form of action, his contract being, to engrave the plate, and to appropriate the prints taken from it to the use of his employer.*

The subjects of engravings are almost always general ones, and cannot be monopolised.   Each particular print is protected by the statutes, but the subject is open to all.†
The prohibition extends only to the piracy of the print ; no exclusive right is created over the picture or common design.

In deciding a question of what is, or what is not, a piracy, Lord Mansfield ‡ says that care must be taken to guard against two extremes equally prejudicial—the one that men of ability, who have employed their time for the service of the community, may not be deprived of their just merits and the reward of their ingenuity and labour; the other that the world may not be deprived of improvements nor the progress of the arts be retarded.   In all

---

* Murray v. Heath 1 B. and Ad. 804.   See P. Albert v. Strange, *ante*, p. 6.
† De Berenger v. Wheble, 2 Stark, 540.
‡ Sayre v. Moore, 1 East, 361, note.

these cases the question of fact to come before the jury is whether the alteration be colourable or not.   In the case of prints, no doubt, different men may take engravings from the same picture.   There is no monopoly of the subject, and upon any question of this nature, the jury will have to decide whether the imitation be servile or not.

In Moore v. Clarke,* an action for pirating an engraving, it was held a correct direction to the jury to consider whether the main design of the plaintiff's engraving had been copied, and whether the defendant's engraving was substantially a copy of the plaintiff's.

The pirate under the Engraving Acts is liable—

1. To penalties, viz. :

    (*a*) To forfeit the plates on which the prints are copied.

    (*b*) To forfeit every sheet on which the work has been printed.

    (*c*) To forfeit 5s. for every print found in his custody ; half to the Queen, half to the informer.

An action for these penalties must be brought within six months; they may also be recovered summarily.†

2. To a special action for damages.

This action must be brought within six years.‡

3. An injunction.§

With regard to the evidence, to be produced by the proprietor, in a proceeding for infringement of copyright in an engraving or etching, lithograph, &c., it is unnecessary to produce the original plate, one of the prints will be sufficient.‖

The proprietor of the copyright in an engraving which is being infringed, who is not also the proprietor of the copyright in the painting from which the engraving is taken, would do well to apply to the owner of the painting, and obtain his consent to be joined as plaintiff in any proceed-

* 9 M. & W., 692.
† See p. 43 *ante*.
‡ Graves v. Mercer, 16 W.R. 790.
§ See p. 55 *post*.
‖ Thompson v. Symonds, 5 T.R. 41, 45.

ings for piracy of the engraving, since the issue of a single print, without the name of the proprietor and the date of publication, would enable any person to make copies of the engraving, by photography or otherwise, with impunity. If, however, there be copyright in the original painting, the owner of the engraving, although he might fail in establishing piracy in the engraving, would succeed on the ground that the copying is, at all events, an infringement of the copyright in the painting, as being a colourable imitation within s. 11 of the Fine Arts Act.* Recent cases have shown how hard it is for an engraver who has not the copyright in the original painting to obtain a conviction as against any pirate but the photographer, it generally turns out that the copy complained of has been taken from the picture itself.

OF THE SUMMARY REMEDY BEFORE JUSTICES.

The 8th section of the Fine Arts Act gives power to the proprietor of copyright in an engraving, etching, &c., to proceed against a pirate before two magistrates ; but the penalties recoverable are only the penalties given under the Engraving Acts,† viz., 5s. for each pirated copy, instead of £10, which is the corresponding penalty for pirating a painting, drawing, or photograph.

These penalties are cumulative ;‡ there should be a separate summons for each sale.

A magistrate sitting within the Metropolitan district, and a stipendiary magistrate elsewhere, or the Lord Mayor, or an Alderman, sitting at the Mansion House or Guildhall, has power, when sitting alone, to exercise the jurisdiction given by the 8th section to two magistrates.§

In Scotland the penalties are recoverable before the Sheriff of the County in which the offence takes place.

* *Exparte* Beal, 3 L.R.Q.B. 388.
† See p. 53 *ante.*
‡ Brooke v. Milliken, 3 T.R. 509. *Exparte* Beal, L.R., 3, Q.B. 388.
§ 2 and 3 Vic., c. 71, s. 14; 11 and 12 Vic., c. 43, ss. 29, 33, 34.

REMEDY BY INJUNCTION.

In addition to the remedies for piracy given by the various statutes dealing with copyright in works of art, the High Court of Justice has jurisdiction in all actions for infringement of copyright to grant injunctions either *interim* or perpetual, in order to prevent further invasion of the right sought to be established.

In applying for an *interim* injunction the claimant must make out a *primâ facie* title, and upon this the injunction issues upon the principle of protecting the property from injury pending the trial of the right by action.

After the establishment of the right by action and of its violation, the successful party is, in general, entitled to a perpetual injunction against the pirate, in order to secure him from the necessity of bringing action upon action in defence of the same right.*

---

* *See* Kerr on injunctions.

CHAPTER VII.

COPYRIGHT IN PAINTINGS, DRAWINGS, AND PHOTO-GRAPHS.

IT seems hardly credible that so recently as the year 1862 no copyright existed in a painting or drawing, yet such is the fact.

" It is a strange anomaly," says Mr. Copinger,* " that while the law gave a property to that which was, in the ordinary way, the work of a man's hands, and allowed a copyright in inventions and designs, it should have afforded no protection to those productions which were exclusively the creations of the mind.   It was thought but an act of justice and right that a copyright should exist in literary productions, but when it was proposed, as late as 1862, to give a similar right to pictures, a cry was raised that it was derogatory on the part of jurisprudence to protect the works of those who contributed by their art to the honour of their country, the elevation of the national taste, and the amusement, instruction, and delight of the community at large."

In 1735 engravings were furnished with statutory protection, yet a painting or drawing of which the engraving was nearly always a mere copy was without any protection until less than twenty years ago.

In an old case, Dr. Berenger v. Wheble,† it appeared that Reinagle had painted two pictures, and that the plaintiff, Dr. Berenger, had purchased the right to engrave them.   Thomson, the engraver, made two sketches from the original pictures, which he disposed of to Wheble, who published them in the " Sporting Magazine."   In an

* " Copinger on Copyright," chapter 14.   † 2 St., N.P. 549.

action by the plaintiff against the defendant, Lord Chief Justice Abbott gave judgment for the defendant, and said " It would destroy all competition in the art to extend the monopoly to the painting itself."

It is as difficult to follow this dictum of the learned judge as it is to understand the opposition to the Bill of 1862 ; but so great was that opposition that the measure had to be smuggled, as it were, through the House. Verbal alterations were needed to make the Act clearer, but, rather than jeopardise its passing, the promoters were advised to allow the Bill to pass in its existing state, and to trust to a future amending Act.   These facts may account for the curious example of legislation called the Fine Arts Act, 1862, the first section of which is about as extraordinary a piece of obscurity as anything in the Statute Law of the Kingdom.

The Act (25 and 26 Vict., c. 68), after reciting that " by law, as now established, the authors of paintings, drawings, and photographs have no copyright in such their works, and it is expedient that the law should in that respect be amended, goes on to enact in s. 1.—"That the author, being a British subject, or resident within the dominions of the Crown, of every original painting, drawing, and photograph, which shall be, or shall have been, made either in the British dominions, or elsewhere, and which shall not have been sold or disposed of before the commencement of this Act (29th July, 1862), and his assigns, shall have the sole and exclusive right of copying, engraving, reproducing, and multiplying such painting or drawing, and the design thereof, or such photograph and the negative thereof, by any means, and of any size, for the term of the natural life of such author, and seven years after his death, provided that when any painting or drawing, or the negative of any photograph, shall, for the first time after the passing of this Act, be sold or disposed of, or shall be made or executed for or on behalf of any other person for a good or a valuable consideration, the person so selling, or disposing of or making, or executing the

same shall not retain the copyright thereof, unless it be expressly reserved to him by agreement in writing, signed at
or before the time of such sale or disposition by the vendee
or assignee of such painting or drawing, or of such negative of a photograph, or by the person for or on whose behalf
the same shall be so made or executed, but the copyright
shall belong to the vendee or assignee of such painting or
drawing, or of such negative of a photograph, or to the
person for or on whose behalf the same shall have been
made or executed ; nor shall the vendee or assignee thereof
be entitled to any such copyright unless at or before the
time of such sale or disposition, an agreement in writing,
signed by the person so selling or disposing of the same,
or by his agent duly authorised, shall have been made to
that effect.''

The practical result of this section is that if an artist
sells a picture—

    (i) Without having the copyright reserved to him by
       written agreement signed by the purchaser ; or

    (ii) Without assigning the copyright to the purchaser
       by written agreement signed, either by himself or by
       his agent duly authorised in writing,

The copyright is lost entirely and cannot be revived.

The only exception is that if the picture has been
painted on commission, instead of being sold after having
been painted, the copyright, in the absence of a written
agreement signed by the person commissioning the work
assigning it to the artist, vests in the person commissioning the work.

The artist should, therefore, be careful, at the time of
sale, or before the time of delivery of the picture, to obtain
the purchaser's signature, or, in the case of commissioned
work, the signature of the person for whom the work has
been, or has to be, done, to a written agreement (Form 1) ;*
or, if he wish to give the copyright to the purchaser, he
should sign Form 2.*   It is better in every case to do one
or the other, rather than to allow the copyright to lapse.

            * See Appendix.

Where work has been executed on commission, and there has been no reservation to the artist, the copyright, upon a sale by the party who commissioned the work, remains in him, unless expressly assigned in writing by him. This should not be forgotten by artists who have worked on commission for picture dealers; they may be enabled to buy back the copyright in their work from the dealer by obtaining his signature to a written assignment thereof.*

The forms given in the Appendix are published separately. The agreement requires a 6d. stamp, and should be taken to Somerset House, and so stamped within 14 days of its being signed; otherwise it cannot be put in evidence at a trial without a penalty of £10 be paid.

Although not absolutely necessary, it is safer to have the agreement stamped. In most cases the certificate of registration † would be sufficient evidence of title, and stamping the agreement is not a condition precedent to registration.

For convenience of reference the copyright owner should keep his copyright agreements and assignments in a book, and affix to each the date of registration.

The right given by the first section of the Fine Arts Act does not affect—

(1) The right of any person to copy any picture which has been published before the Act, or since that time, without the conditions of Section 1 having been carried out.

(2) The right of any person to make a painting, drawing, or photograph of any scene or object which someone else has already painted, drawn, or photographed, and in which the latter has obtained copyright.‡

An artist may obtain a monopoly of his design—*i.e.*, treatment of a subject, but not of the subject itself.

Sec. 3.—By this section copyright is made personal property, and every assignment and every license to copy §

---

* See Appendix.
† S. 5 of Fine Arts Act, 1862.
‡ Sec. 2, Appendix.
§ Form 5, Appendix.

must be in writing, signed by the proprietor, or by his agent appointed for that purpose in writing.*

Upon the death of the proprietor copyright passes, without mention under his will, as part of the residuary personal estate, and goes to the next-of-kin in case of intestacy.   On bankruptcy it vests in the trustee.

If a person has a copyright, he may give a license to copy, but the giving of such a license is not an assignment of the copyright in the original.   The copyist acquires copyright in his own work only when finished.†

Thus an artist who has secured the copyright of his picture may give such a license to the editor of a periodi-cal—*e.g.*, to make a woodcut—and he does not thereby transfer his copyright to such editor.

REGISTRATION OF PAINTINGS, DRAWINGS, AND PHOTOGRAPHS.

IT is a very common error to suppose that it is registra-tion which creates copyright in paintings, drawings, and photographs.   There can be no greater mistake made. Registration does not confer any title to copyright; it is merely a condition precedent to the proprietor's right to sue, and it also enables him to prove his title in an easy manner.

The proprietor of copyright in a painting, drawing, or photograph cannot sue for piracy until he registers, and then only for piracy after registration.

The proprietor of a mere license to copy a painting in a particular way is not entitled to register the copyright in the painting; he can only register the copyright in his copy when made—*e.g.*, the owner of the license to photo-graph a painting could not register the painting, but only his photograph.

* Form 8, Appendix.
† Lucas v. Cooke; see p. 61.

In the recent case of Lucas v. Cooke* there was an agreement signed by Mr. Halford, and addressed to the plaintiff in these words—" I assign to you, for the purpose of producing an engraving of one size, the copyright of the picture painted by Mr. W. V. Eddis, entitled ' Going to Work,' and being a portrait of my daughter."

The plaintiff registered the copyright in the original painting, and contended that, by the agreement, he was entitled to the whole copyright in the painting, notwithstanding the words limiting the effect of it, and that, at all events, the registration being *primâ facie* evidence of title conveyed to him as against all the world, except Mr. Halford, the absolute copyright in the painting. But the very document which he produced in evidence rebutted this *primâ facie* title, for it showed that it was impossible that he could have the whole copyright. It is difficult to see why Mr. Lucas resorted to the register at all in this case,† for the agreement, although it contained the words " assign " and " copyright," was a mere license to engrave, which imparted a right to secure copyright in the engraving when finished, and registration is not necessary in order to secure copyright in an engraving.

The following is a summary of the law with regard to the registration of copyright in paintings, drawings, and photographs :—

A book, entitled the " Register of Proprietors of Copyright in Paintings, Drawings, and Photographs," must be kept at the Hall of the Stationers' Company.‡

A memorandum of any copyright to which any person is entitled under s. 1 of the Fine Arts Act, and of every subsequent assignment of any such copyright, must be entered therein. Such memorandum must contain a statement of—

(*a*) The date of the agreement or assignment.

* L.R. xiii, Ch. Div.
† See Dialogue, p. 15.
‡ S. 4, Appendix.

(*b*) The names of the parties thereto.

(*c*) The name and address of the person in whom such copyright is vested in virtue thereof, and of the author of the work.

(*d*) A short description of the nature and subject of such work, and, if the person registering so desires, a sketch, outline, or photograph of the work in addition thereto.

No proprietor of any such copyright is entitled to the benefit of The Fine Arts Act, 1862, until such registration, and no action can be maintained, nor any penalty recovered, in respect of anything done before registration.* But it is not necessary to the validity of a registered assignment that previous assignments should be registered.

Any person aggrieved by any such entry may apply to the High Court, or any judge thereof, to have such entry expunged or varied, and the Court may make such entry as it thinks just.

It is a misdemeanour to make or cause to be made any false entry in such book wilfully.†

The officer in charge of the book is bound to give sealed and certified copies of the entries contained therein on payment of a fee of 5s., and such copies are *primâ facie* proof of the matters alleged therein.

The fee for registration is one shilling; the search fee also one shilling. Forms can be obtained at the office for one penny each. A copy of the form is given in the Appendix. It must be signed by the proprietor of copyright, and should be taken—not sent—to the office by some trustworthy person.

Copyright may be registered at any time, but it ought to be done at once, otherwise a piracy may go unpunished. Where copyright has been assigned more than once, the proprietor may register it without mentioning either the original, or any of the prior assignments, but all subse-

---

* Graves' Case, L.R., 4 Q.B., 715.

† 5 and 6 Vic., c. 45, s. 11, 12, and 14, extended by s. 5 of Fine Arts Act. See Appendix.

quent assignments must be registered, the reason being that any one may trace out the proprietorship. The assignee of a registered copyright should therefore register immediately. With regard to the description of the work, the object of the Legislature, as pointed out by the Act, is that there shall be such description as to enable a person who has the picture or work before him to judge whether or not the registration applies to the one he is about to copy.

In Beal's case* Lord Blackburn says :—" In all cases it would be a question of fact whether the description is sufficient to point out the picture registered. The picture ' Ordered on Foreign Service' represents an officer, who is ordered abroad, taking leave of a lady, and no one can doubt that is the picture intended. So, again, ' My First Sermon' describes with sufficient exactness a child, impressed with the novelty of her situation, sitting in a pew and listening with her eyes open ; while the same child, fast asleep in a pew, forms the subject of ' My Second Sermon.' Who can doubt that in each of these cases the description is sufficient ? There may be a few instances in which the registration of the name of the picture is not sufficient ; for instance, Sir Edwin Landseer's picture of a Newfoundland dog might possibly be insufficiently registered under the description of ' A Distinguished Member of the Humane Society.' Similarly, a well-known picture called ' A Piper and a Pair of Nut-crackers,' representing a bullfinch and a pair of squirrels, might not be accurately pointed out by its name. In either of these cases the names would scarcely be sufficient, and it would be advisable for a person proposing to register them to add a sketch or outline of the work."

In case of commissioned work, if the registration be made by the person who commissioned the work, he should leave a blank space, under " Date of Agreement," and " Names of Parties," or write, " Painted on Commission."

A person to be "aggrieved" must show that the entry in

* 3 L.R.Q.B., 393.

the register is inconsistent with some right which he sets up in himself or in some other person, or that the entry would really interfere with some intended action on the part of the person making the application.   For instance, if a person brought to the notice of the Court that he had a right to take copies of certain pictures but was afraid to do so while the entry existed, he would be a person "aggrieved" within the meaning of the section. *

* Chappell v. Purday, 11 M. & W., 303; Graves Case, L.R. 4, Q. Bench, 715.

CHAPTER VIII.

PIRACY OF PAINTINGS, DRAWINGS, AND PHOTOGRAPHS.

THE manner in which the chief piracies of paintings are made is as follows :—

(1) Piratical copies are made abroad, and imported into this country for sale.

(2) Photographs or lithographs of engravings made from a picture are hawked about.

(3) Copies of paintings are made, signed, and sold as originals.

(4) The style of a particular painter is imitated, and his signature forged.

Artists complain that the present law is powerless to put an end to these forms of piracy.   The fault is rather with themselves.   A perusal of the Fine Arts Act will show that the law gives a remedy in each case, but artists will not avail themselves of it, on the ground that proceedings waste their time and involve them in expense.   So does the protection of all property.   Let artists and publishers combine to enforce the law.   An association, with a lawyer at its head, and with two or three sharp agents under him, would soon root out the evil.*

The following is a summary of the provisions of the Fine Arts Act, 1862, with regard to piracy :—

Every one (including the author when he is not the proprietor) commits an offence who, without the consent of the proprietor of the copyright therein, does any of the following things with regard to any painting, drawing, or photograph, in which copyright exists :—

(a) Repeats, copies, colourably imitates, or otherwise multiplies for sale, hire, exhibition, or distribution, any such work, or the design thereof.

* See Dialogue, p. 23 *ante.*

F

(*b*) Causes or procures to be done anything mentioned in *a*.

(*c*) Sells, publishes, lets to hire, exhibits or distributes, offers for any such purposes, imports into the United Kingdom any such repetition, copy, or other imitation of any such work, or of the design thereof, knowing that it has been unlawfully made.

(*d*) Causes or procures to be done anything mentioned in (*c*).

Every one, whether the owner of copyright or not, commits an offence who—

(*e*) Fraudulently signs, or otherwise affixes, or fraudulently causes to be signed, or otherwise affixed to or upon any painting, drawing, or photograph, or the negative thereof, any name, initials, or monogram.

(*f*) Fraudulently sells, publishes, exhibits, or disposes of, or offers for sale, exhibition, or distribution any painting, drawing, or photograph, or the negative of a photograph, having thereon the name, initials, or monogram of a person who did not execute or make such a work.

(*g*) Fraudulently utters, disposes of, or puts off, or causes to be uttered or disposed of, any copy or colourable imitation of any painting, drawing, or photograph, or negative of a photograph, whether there is subsisting copyright therein or not, as having been made or executed by the author or maker of the original work from which such copy or imitation has been taken.

(*h*) Makes, or knowingly sells, publishes, or offers for sale any painting, drawing, or photograph which, after being sold or parted with by the author or maker thereof, has been altered by any other person by addition or otherwise, or any copy of such work so altered, or of any part thereof, as the unaltered work of such author or maker during his life or without his consent.

Every one who commits any of the offences (*a*), (*b*), (*c*), or (*d*) forfeits to the proprietor of the copyright for the

time being a sum not exceeding £10,* and all such repetitions, copies, and imitations made without such consent
as aforesaid, and all negatives of photographs made for the
purpose of obtaining such copies.

Every one who commits any of the offences (e), (f), (g),
or (h) forfeits to the person aggrieved a sum not exceeding
£10, or double the price, if any, at which all such copies,
engravings, imitations, or altered works were sold or
offered for sale; and all such copies, engravings, and imitations and altered works are forfeited to the person whose
name, initial, or monogram are fraudulently signed or
affixed, or to whom such spurious or altered work is
fraudulently or falsely ascribed; provided that none of the
last-mentioned penalties are incurred unless the person to
whom such spurious or altered work is so fraudulently
ascribed, or whose name, initial, or monogram is so fraudulently or falsely ascribed was living at or within twenty
years next before the time when the offence was committed.†

The penalties hereinbefore specified are cumulative, ‡
and the person aggrieved by any of the acts before mentioned may recover damages in addition to such penalties,
and may in any case recover and enforce the delivery to
him of the things specified, and recover damages for their
retention or conversion.

The penalties may be recovered either by action or
before two justices or a stipendiary magistrate.§   There
is also the remedy by injunction.‖

The importation into the United Kingdom of repetitions, copies, or imitations of paintings, drawings, or photographs wherein, or in the design whereof, there is an
existing copyright under 25 and 26 Vic., c. 68, or of the
design thereof, or of the negatives of photographs, is
absolutely prohibited, except by the consent of the pro-

* 25 and 26 Vic., c. 68. s. 6.
† 25 and 26 Vic., c. 68, s. 7.   Steph. Dig.
‡ Brooke v. Milliken, 3 T.R., 509; ex parte Beal, L.R. 3, Q.B., 395.
§ 25 and 26 Vic., c. 68, s. 8; 2 and 3 Vic., c. 71, s. 14; 11 and 12
Vic., c. 43, ss. 29, 33, 34.   See p. 54 ante.
‖ Ante p. 55.

68   THE LAW OF ARTISTIC COPYRIGHT.

prietor of the copyright or his agent authorised in writing.*

What is a copy? The definition given in the case of West v. Frances is that "a copy is that which comes so near to the original as to give every person seeing it the idea created by the original."† The correctness of this definition has been doubted,‡ and in *ex parte* Beal§ a more tangible explanation is given of the construction to be put upon the word as used in the 6th section of the Act. Lord Blackburn there says:—"The copyright in the picture belongs to Mr. Graves. He made an engraving of it, of which he sold copies. He had not given any right to others to multiply them, and the photographs for which the penalties were recovered were made by photographing the engraving, and not the original picture; and it has been argued that the photograph of the engraving, being a reproduction of a copy of the design of the painting, is not a copy of the painting itself. It seems to me that cannot be so. When the subject of a picture is copied, it is of no consequence whether that is done directly from the picture itself, or through intervening copies. If in the result that which is copied be an imitation of the picture, then it is immaterial whether that be arrived at directly or by intermediate steps. A doubt was suggested by the Court whether there might not be a difficulty arising upon the wording of s. 6,‖ whether the enactment might merely mean the imitation of a painting by a painting, of a drawing by a drawing, and of a photograph by a photograph, and that a photograph of a drawing would not be within the meaning of the Legislature. But when we look at the 1st section,¶ which is the key to the whole

* Fine Arts Act, s. 10.
† 5 B. and A., 737.
‡ In Dicks v. Brooks, L.R. xv., Ch. Div., 29. Bacon V.C. says:— "The definition read from West v. Francis I should not adopt exclusively and conclusively as applying to every case, although it applies perfectly to the case in which it was used."
§ L.R. 3, Q.B. 393.
‖ See Appendix.
¶ *Ante,* p. 36.

Act, the terms used are so extensive that it is plain that a photograph of a painting, of a drawing, or of another photograph, made without the consent of the owner, though of a different size, *provided it be a reproduction of the design,* is such an infringement as would subject the maker to the penalty."

At common law it had been decided in 1857* that to sign a painter's name to a picture which has not been painted by him is no forgery. The person doing so cannot be indicted for forging or uttering the forged name of the painter, for the crime of forgery must be committed with reference to some document or writing, and does not extend to the fraudulent imitation of a name put on a picture merely as a mark to identify it as the painter's work ; but if a person knowingly sells as an original, a copy of a picture, with the painter's name imitated upon it, and, by means of the imitated name, knowingly and fraudulently induce another to buy and pay for the picture as a genuine work of the artist, he may be indicted as a cheat by means of a false token at common law independently of s. 7 of the Act† which now covers such a case.

With regard to the piratical copies which are hawked about the country, and particularly photographs of copyright paintings and engravings, the power given to proceed by summons has at present proved ineffectual to stop the traffic, because the persons selling these copies go round from house to house, and refuse to give either a name or address, and are gone before a summons can be procured.

In the Report of Copyright Commission there is a recommendation that in any future Act a clause to the effect that "all such unlawful articles may be seized without warrant by any peace officer under the orders and responsibility of the proprietor of the copyright, or any person authorised by him," &c. In the Bill now before the House of Commons‡ a similar clause is inserted.

* R. v. Closs, 27 L.J.M.C., 54.
† See Appendix.
‡ See Appendix.

CHAPTER IX.

COPYRIGHT IN SCULPTURE AND BUSTS, MODELS, &c.

THE Act upon which copyright in sculpture depends is 54 Geo. III., c. 56 ;* an earlier statute (38 Geo. III., c. 71) being now repealed.

The plastic art may, at present, be copied by the graphic art. There is no protection afforded to the sculptor against paintings, drawings, engravings, or photographs; copyright in a work of sculpture, whether commissioned or not, belongs to the sculptor, provided he complies with the requirements of the Sculpture Act, the material provisions of which are as follows :—

Every person who makes, or causes to be made, any new and original sculpture, or model, or copy, or cast of—

(1) The human figure.

(2) Any bust.

(3) Any part of the human figure clothed in drapery or otherwise.

(4) Any animal.

(5) Any part of an animal combined with the human figure or otherwise.

(6) Any subject, being matter of invention in sculpture.

(7) Any alto or basso-relievo, representing any of the matters above-mentioned.

(8) Any cast from nature.

    (a) of the human figure.

    (b) of any part or parts of the human figure.

    (c) of any animal.

    (d) of any parts of the animal.

    (e) of any such subject (*i.e.*, being matter of inven-

* See Appendix.

tion in sculpture), containing or representing any
of the things hereinbefore-mentioned, whether
separate or combined,

has the sole right and property therein for the term of 14
years from the first putting forth or publishing the same,
provided that the proprietor causes his name with the date
to be put on all and every such new and original sculpture,
model, copy, or cast before it is published.*

"This section," says Mr. Justice Stephen,† "is a
miracle of intricacy and verbosity. It contains an 'of'
which may be a misprint, as it seems to make nonsense of
several lines, and a most puzzling 'such,' of which I have
given a conjectural interpretation. Moreover, every sub-
stantive is given both in the singular and the plural—
'figure or figures,' 'part or parts,' &c., &c. The section
forms a sentence of 38 lines ; the first half of which is repeated in the second half in so intricate a way that the
draftsman appears to have lost himself in the middle of
it. It admits of a doubt whether a cast from nature of an
animal is the subject of copyright at all, and whether it
must not be a cast from a cast from nature."

If the proprietor be living at the end of the term of 14
years his right returns to him for a further term of 14
years, unless he has divested himself thereof.

The very letter of the law must be complied with. In
order to acquire copyright the sculptor must engrave, not
only on the finished work, but on every model, copy, or
cast prepared by him in the process of making it, his name,
and the day of the month and year when the work is first
shown, and such date must not be altered.

Statues and models, and everything that comes within
the Act, may be registered at the office for the Registration
of Designs, now the office of the Commissioners of
Patents.‡

The proprietor shall give such copy, drawing, print, or

---

* 54 Geo. III., c. 56, ss. 1 and 6. See Appendix.
† Digest appended to Copyright Commissioners' Report, 1878.
‡ 13 and 14 Vic., c. 104, s. 6. See Appendix.

description of his work as shall in the judgment of the Registrar be sufficient to identify it, and the name of the proprietor and his address. The Registrar of Designs shall then grant a certificate of such registration.

A photograph would answer the purpose of this section better than a description of the piece of sculpture.

The application to register can be made by the proprietor for the time being as well as by the author.

Every copy or cast of such sculpture, model, copy or cast, which shall be published by the proprietor after registration, must be marked with the word "registered," and with the date of registration.*

The effect of registration, under the Designs Act,† is to add penalties for piracy to the right of action for damages given by the Sculpture Act.‡ For every offence the pirate is to forfeit to the proprietor a sum of not less than £5 and not exceeding £30.

These penalties are recoverable either by action of debt or summarily before justices.§ In the latter case the aggregate amount of penalties recoverable for offences, in respect of any one design committed by any one person, is limited to the sum of £100.

Copyright in sculpture can only be assigned by deed, and attested by two witnesses. A form is given in the Appendix, but the assignor will probably need the services of a professional man in order to carry out an assignment.

The action for damages under the Sculpture Act must be commenced within six months after the commission of the offence; that for penalties within twelve months. ||

With regard to sculpture, the Report of the Royal Commission is as follows :—

"We are disposed to think that every form of copy,

---

* 13 and 14 Vic., c. 104, s. 7.   See Appendix.
† Ib.
‡ 54 Geo. III., c. 56, s. 3.
§ 5 and 6 Vic., c. 100, s. 8.   13 and 14 Vic., c. 104, s. 7.
|| 5 and 6 Vic., c. 100, s. 12.

whether by sculpture, modelling, photography, drawing, engraving, or otherwise, should be included in the protection of copyright. It might be provided that the copying of a scene, in which a piece of sculpture happened to form an object, should not be deemed an infringement, unless the sculpture should be the principal object, or unless the chief purpose of the picture should be to exhibit the sculpture. It was also suggested that copyists of antique works ought to be protected by copyright as far as their own copies are concerned. Many persons spend months in copying ancient statues, and the copies become as valuable to the sculptors as if they were original works. It may be doubted whether the case does not already fall within the Sculpture Act ; but we recommend that such doubts should be removed, and that sculptors who copy from statues in which no copyright exists should have copyright in their own copies. Such copyright should not, of course, extend to prevent other persons making copies of the original work."

ARCHITECTURE.

At present there is no copyright in an architectural design farther than that it is protected as a drawing by the Fine Arts Act, 1862, and so may not be copied on paper. In justice, it would seem that the design of a building should be as much entitled to protection as that of a statue. Mr. Charles Barry, the President of the Royal Institute of British Architects, gave evidence before the Copyright Commission in February, 1877, and suggested that the right to reproduce a building should be reserved to the architect for 20 years ; and further that copyright in architectural designs should be reserved to the author from the date of the erection of a building, or the sale of the design. His suggestions were, however, rejected, on the ground, as the Report of the Commissioners states, that it would be impossible to carry them out in practice.

If the architect wishes to acquire copyright in his drawings he should be careful to carry out the practical suggestions as to the signing of the memorandum and registration, to be found in the Chapters on Copyright in Paintings, Drawings, and Photographs.

CHAPTER X.

INTERNATIONAL COPYRIGHT.

COPYRIGHT in works of art first published in foreign countries is granted to the authors of such works in the manner, to the extent, and on the terms following, if what the Government of this country regards as due protection has been secured by the foreign country, in which such works are first published, for the benefit of persons interested in similar works first published in British dominions.*

Her Majesty may, by Order in Council, direct that the authors of any works of art, being first published in such foreign country, shall have copyright therein under the Engraving, Sculpture, and Fine Arts Acts, but no author of any such foreign work of art is entitled to any benefit under the provisions of the International Copyright Act, unless the work is registered at Stationers' Hall.†

A foreign print or engraving must have the name of the proprietor and date of first publication engraved on the plate and printed on each print.‡

The importation into any part of the British dominions of copies of any work of art, the copyright of which has been protected by the provisions of the Act, is absolutely prohibited, unless by the consent of the registered proprietor or by that of his agent authorised in writing.§

Notwithstanding great exertions that have from time to time been made, it has hitherto been found impracticable to arrange any terms of reciprocal protection with the

---

* 7 and 8 Vic., c. 12, s. 2, included in Fine Arts Act, 1862 ; 15 and 16 Vic., c. 12.

† For a form of registration, see Appendix.

‡ Alvanzo v. Mudie, 10 Exch., 203.

§ 15 and 16 Vic., c. 12, s. 9.

American people, the result being, that an English artist, or publisher, has no remedy whatever against the piracy of his works in the United States. The works of British authors and painters may be, and generally are, taken without leave by American publishers—sometimes mutilated, issued at a cheap rate to a population of nearly fifty millions of people, who are, perhaps, the most active readers in the world, and not seldom in forms that are most objectionable to the feelings of the original artist or author.

The reason for this deplorable state of things is not far to seek. The original works published in America are less numerous than our own. Thus the American publisher is tempted to take advantage of the works of the older country, and at the same time is induced to curtail the publication of original works of his own land. The American author also has not the same need of a convention as the English, since our law affords copyright protection throughout the British dominions to foreigners as well as to British subjects provided they publish their works in the United Kingdom before bringing them out elsewhere, while the American law, unlike ours, does not make first publication at home a condition of obtaining copyright. It is consequently the practice of some American authors to publish their works first in the United Kingdom, and so to obtain British copyright, and then to republish them in the United States, and obtain American copyright, or to publish in the two countries almost simultaneously.*

The reasons above given show the difficulties which lie in the way of a satisfactory solution of the question, although as a matter of fact they relate to books more than to works of art, except illustrations contained in books. By a temporary residence in the United Kingdom an American artist can obtain copyright here in his painting, and then he can obtain copyright in his own country.

The Copyright Commissioners are adverse to the taking

* See Report of Copyright Commissioners.

of any measures of a retaliatory character, such as the withdrawal from the Americans of the privilege of copyright on first publication in this country, and they recommend the appointment of a mixed commission to examine and report upon the whole subject with a view to the arrangement of the terms of a copyright convention between the two nations.

France.

' By the Convention of 1851, and a decree of 1852, the works of English authors published out of France are protected, and an Englishman who publishes a work of art in France may, by complying with the law of France, acquire copyright for his own life, and for fifty years after his death, on condition that he deposits in the National Library a copy of the work, for otherwise he will not be able to proceed for piracy of his copyright.

Copyright conventions have been arranged with most of the nations of the European Continent, whereby reciprocal protection has been secured for the authors of those countries and for British subjects.   To mention the copyright laws of those countries is beyond the province of a handbook, and the reader is referred to the larger works on the subject which are to be found in our legal libraries.

Colonial Copyright.

The Acts relating to copyright in works of the fine arts apply to all the British dominions.*   With regard to Canada, the British artist's position is regulated by an Act passed by the Dominion Parliament in 1875,† which gives copyright for 28 years to any person, domiciled in Canada, or in any part of the British possessions, or being

* The Imperial statutes relating to Colonial Copyright are 5 and 6 Vic., c. 45; 10 and 11 Vic., c. 95; 16 and 17 Vic., c. 107; and 18 and 19 Vic., c. 96; and the Canada Copyright Act, 1875, 38 and 39 Vic., c. 53.   The latter, however, is the only one of these Acts which relates to works of art.

† The Canadian Act, 1875, is given in the schedule to the 38 and 39 Vic., c. 53.

a citizen of any country having an International Copy-right Treaty with the United Kingdom, who is the author of any original painting, drawing, statue, sculpture, or photograph, or who invents, designs, etches, or engraves, or causes to be engraved, etched, or made from his own design any print or engraving, and to the legal representa-tives of such person.

This is subject to the condition that the work of art be produced or reproduced in Canada. ˙ Such production or reproduction may be previous to, contemporaneous with,˙ or subsequent to publication elsewhere, but the copyright is not to continue in Canada after it has expired anywhere else. If at the expiration of the 28 years the author is still living, or has died and left a widow or child, a further period of fourteen years for copyright accrues to him or them.

The person desirous of obtaining such copyright must deposit with the Minister of Agriculture two copies of a photograph, print, cut, or engraving, and in the case of paintings, drawings, statuary and sculpture a written de-scription of the work, and the copyright will then be recorded.

Upon every photograph, print, cut, or engraving must be impressed, on its face, the words, " Entered according to Act of Parliament of Canada, in the year ——, by A. B., in the Office of the Minister of Agriculture." But as re-gards paintings, drawings, statuary, and sculptures, the signature of the artist will suffice.

Interim copyright, pending the production or reproduc-tion in Canada, can be obtained to last for a month.

CHAPTER XI.

THE STATUTE OF FRAUDS.

A CONTRACT to paint a picture, or to execute a work of art on commission, for a price of £10 or upwards, and a contract for the sale of a work of art, is a contract within the 17th section of 29 Car. II, c. 3, and is therefore not enforceable unless one of three things take place—

(1) The purchaser must accept the work of art and actually receive it; or

(2) The purchaser must give something in earnest to bind the bargain, or in part payment; or

(3) Some note or memorandum of the bargain must be made, and signed by the party to be charged therewith or his agent.

An artist should therefore obtain a small cheque or payment on account, or obtain the commissioner's signature to a document stating the material terms of the agreement, otherwise the purchaser may refuse to accept the work of art when completed, or to pay for it.

On the other hand, the commissioner or purchaser would do well to obtain the signature of the artist to a similar document, or to pay him something on account, or he may be kept waiting by a dilatory artist, or not obtain his work of art at all.

In the case of Lee v. Griffin,* which was an action for the price of a set of artificial teeth, it was objected on behalf of the defendant, that where the chief part of what is supplied is the skill, the contract is not for the sale of goods within the Statute of Frauds. Lord Blackburn said:—" Here, if the teeth had been delivered and accepted,

* 30 L.J.Q.B., 254.

the contract for the sale of a chattel would have been complete. I do not think the relative value of the labour, and of the materials on which it is bestowed, can in any case be the test of what is the cause of action ; and that if Benvenuto Cellini had contracted to execute a work of art for another, much as the value of the skill might exceed that of the materials, the contract would have been the less for the sale of a chattel."

If time be not mentioned in an agreement for the execution and delivery of a work of art, the artist is bound to deliver it within a reasonable time.

The agreement above mentioned is, of course, altogether independent of the question of copyright.

APPENDIX.

8 George II., c. 13 (1735).

An Act for the Encouragement of the Art of Designing, Engraving, and Etching Historical and other Prints, by vesting the Properties thereof in the Inventors and Engravers during the time therein mentioned.

WHEREAS divers persons have, by their own genius, industry, pains, and expense, invented and engraved, or worked in mezzotinto, or chiaro-oscuro, sets of historical and other prints, in hopes to have reaped the sole benefit of their labours: And whereas printsellers and other persons have of late, without the consent of the inventors, designers, and proprietors of such prints, frequently taken the liberty of copying, engraving, and publishing, or causing to be copied, engraved and published, base copies of such works, designs, and prints, to the very great prejudice and detriment of the inventors, designers, and proprietors thereof: For remedy thereof, and for preventing such practices for the future, may it please Your Majesty that it be enacted ; and be it enacted by the King's most excellent Majesty, by and with the advice and consent of the Lords spiritual and temporal, and Commons, in this present Parliament assembled, and by the authority of the same, That from and after the twenty-fourth day of June, which shall be in the year of our Lord one thousand seven hundred and thirty-five, every person who shall invent and design, engrave, etch, or work, in mezzotinto or chiaro-oscuro, or from his own works and invention shall cause to be designed and engraved, etched, or worked, in mezzotinto or chiaro-oscuro, any historical or other print or

G

prints, shall have the sole right and liberty of printing and reprinting the same for the term of fourteen years, to commence from the day of the first publishing thereof, which shall be truly engraved with the name of the proprietor on each plate, and printed on every such print or prints; and that if the printseller or other person whatsoever, from and after the said twenty-fourth day of June, one thousand seven hundred and thirty-five, within the time limited by this Act, shall engrave, etch, or work as aforesaid, or in any other manner copy and sell, or cause to be engraved, etched, or copied and sold, in the whole or in part, by varying, adding to, or diminishing from the main design, or shall print, reprint, or import for sale, or cause to be printed, reprinted, or imported for sale, any such print or prints, or any parts thereof, without the consent of the proprietor or proprietors thereof, first had and obtained in writing, signed by him or them respectively, in the presence of two or more credible witnesses; or, knowing the same to be so printed or reprinted, without the consent of the proprietor or proprietors, shall publish, sell, or expose to sale, or otherwise, or in any other manner dispose of or cause to be published, sold, or exposed to sale or otherwise, or in any other manner disposed of, any such print or prints, without such consent first, had and obtained as aforesaid, then such offender or offenders shall forfeit the plate or plates on which such print or prints are, or shall be copied, and all and every sheet or sheets (being part of, or whereon such print or prints are or shall be so copied or printed), to the proprietor or proprietors of such original print or prints, who shall forthwith destroy and damask the same; and further, that every such offender or offenders shall forfeit five shillings for every print which shall be found in his, her, or their custody, either printed or published, and exposed to sale or otherwise disposed of, contrary to the true intent and meaning of this Act, the one moiety thereof to the King's most excellent Majesty, his heirs and successors, and the other moiety thereof to any person or persons that shall sue for the same, to be recovered in any of His Majesty's Courts of Record at Westminster, by action of debt, bill, plaint, or information in which no wager of law, essoign, privilege, or protection, or more than one imparlance, shall be allowed.

II. Provided nevertheless, That it shall and may be lawful for any person or persons who shall hereafter purchase any plate or plates for printing from the original proprietors thereof to print and reprint from the said plates without incurring any of the penalties in this Act mentioned.

III. And be it further enacted by the authority aforesaid, That if any action or suit shall be commenced or brought against any person or persons whatsoever for doing or causing to be done anything in pursuance of this Act, the same shall be brought within the space of three months after so doing; and the defendant and defendants in such action or suit shall, or may, plead the general issue, and give the special matter in evidence; and if upon such action or suit a verdict shall be given for the defendant or defendants, or if the plaintiff or plaintiffs become nonsuited, or discontinue his, her, or their action or actions, then the defendant or defendants shall have and recover full costs for the recovery whereof he shall have the same remedy as any other defendant or defendants in any other case hath or have by law.

IV. Provided always, and be it further enacted by the authority aforesaid, That if any action or suit shall be commenced or brought against any person or persons for any offence committed against this Act, the same shall be brought within the space of three months after the discovery of every such offence, and not afterwards, anything in this Act contained to the contrary notwithstanding.

V. Repealed by 30 and 31 Vict., c. 59.

VI. And be it further enacted by the authority aforesaid, That this Act shall be deemed, adjudged, and taken to be a Public Act, and be judicially taken notice of as such by all judges, justices, and other persons whatsoever, without especially pleading the same.

7 George III. c. 38 (1766).

An Act to amend and render more effectual an Act made in the Eighth Year of the Reign of King George the Second, for Encouragement of the Acts of designing, engraving, and etching historical and other Prints; and for vesting, in and securing to, Jane Hogarth, Widow, the Property in certain Prints.

WHEREAS an Act of Parliament passed in the eighth year of the reign of His late Majesty King George the Second, intituled "An Act for the Encouragement of the Arts of designing, engraving, and etching historical and other Prints, by vesting the Properties thereof in the Inventors and Engravers, during the time therein mentioned," has been found ineffectual for the purposes thereby intended: Be it enacted that the King's most excellent Majesty, by and with the advice and consent of the Lord's spiritual and temporal, and Commons, in this present Parliament assembled, and by the authority of the same, that from and after the first day of January, one thousand seven hundred and sixty-seven, all and every person or persons who shall invent or design, engrave, etch, or work mezzotinto or chiaro-oscuro, or, from his own work, design, or invention, shall cause or procure to be designed, engraved, etched, or worked in mezzotinto or chiaro-oscuro, any historical print or prints, or any print or prints of any portrait, conversation, landscape, or architecture, map, chart, or plan or any other print or prints whatsoever, shall have, and are hereby declared to have, the benefit and protection of the said Act and this Act, under the restrictions and limitations hereinafter mentioned.

II. And be it further enacted by the authority aforesaid, That from and after the said first day of January, one thousand seven hundred and sixty-seven, all and every person and persons who shall engrave, etch, or work in mezzotinto or chiaro-oscuro, or cause to be engraved, etched, or worked any print taken from any picture, drawing, model, or sculpture, either ancient or modern, shall have, and are hereby declared to have, the benefit and protection of the said Act and this Act, for the term hereinafter mentioned, in like manner as if such print had been graved or drawn from the original design of such graver, etcher, or draftsman; and if any person shall engrave, print, or publish, or import for sale, any copy of such print, contrary to the true intent and meaning of this and the said former Act, every such person shall be liable to the penalties contained in the said Act, to be recovered as therein and hereinafter is mentioned.

III. and IV. repealed by 30 and 31 Vict., c. 59.

V. And be it further enacted by the authority aforesaid, That all and every the penalties and penalty inflicted by the said Act and extended, and meant to be extended, to the several cases comprised in this Act shall and may be sued for and recovered in like manner and under the like restrictions and limitations as in and by the said Act is declared and appointed; and the plaintiff or common informer in every such action (in case such plaintiff or common informer shall recover any of the penalties incurred by this or the said former Act) shall recover the same, together with full costs of suit. Provided, also, that the party prosecuting shall commence his prosecution within the space of six calendar months after the offence committed.

VI. And be it further enacted by the authority aforesaid, That the sole right and liberty of printing and reprinting intended to be secured and protected by the said former Act and this Act, shall be extended, continued, and be vested in the respective proprietors, for the space of twenty-eight days, to commence from the day of the first publishing of any of the works respectively hereinbefore, and in the said former Act mentioned.

VII. And be it further enacted by the authority aforesaid, That if any action or suit shall be commenced or brought against any person or persons whatsoever, for doing, or causing to be done, anything in pursuance of this Act, the same shall be brought within the space of six

calendar months after the fact committed ; and the defendant or defendants in any such action or suit shall or
may plead the general issue, and give the special matter
in evidence ; and if, upon such action or suit a verdict shall
be given for the defendant or defendants, or if the plaintiff
or plaintiffs become non-suited, or discontinue his, her, or
their action or actions, then the defendant or defendants
shall have and recover full costs ; for the recovery whereof
he shall have the same remedy as any other defendant or
defendants in any other case, hath or have by law.

17 George III., c. 57 (1777).

*An Act for more effectually securing the Property of
Prints to Inventors and Engravers by enabling them to
sue for and recover Penalties in certain cases.*

WHEREAS an Act of Parliament passed in the eighth
year of the reign of His late Majesty King George the
Second, intituled " An Act for the Encouragement of the
Arts of designing, engraving, and etching historical and
other Prints, by vesting the Properties thereof in the
Inventors and Engravers during the Time therein mentioned : " And whereas, by an Act of Parliament passed
in the seventh year of the reign of His present Majesty
for amending and rendering more effectual the aforesaid
Act, and for other purposes therein mentioned, it was
(among other things) enacted, That from and after the
first day of January one thousand seven hundred and
sixty seven, all and every person or persons who shall
engrave, etch, or work in mezzotinto or chiaro-oscuro, or
caused to be engraved, etched, or worked, any print taken
from any picture, drawing, model, or sculpture, either
ancient or modern, should have, and were thereby declared
to have the benefit and protection of the said former Act
and that Act, for the term thereinafter mentioned, in like
manner as if such print had been graved or drawn from
the original design of such graver, etcher, or draughtsman ;
and whereas the said Acts had not effectually answered

the purposes for which they were intended, and it is necessary for the encouragement of artists, and for securing to
them the property of and in their works, and for the
advancement and improvement of the aforesaid arts, that
such further provisions should be made as are hereinafter
mentioned and contained: May it therefore please your
Majesty that it may be enacted; and be it enacted by the
King's most excellent Majesty, by and with the advice
and consent of the Lords spiritual and temporal, and
Commons, in this present Parliament assembled, and by
the authority of the same, That from and after the twenty-
fourth day of June, one thousand seven hundred and
seventy-seven, if any engraver, etcher, print seller or
other person shall, within the time limited by the aforesaid Acts, or either of them, engrave, etch, or work, or
cause or procure to be engraved, etched, or worked in
mezzotinto or chiaro-oscuro, or otherwise, or in any other
manner copy, in the whole or in part, by varying, adding to,
or diminishing from the main design, or shall print, reprint, or import for sale, or cause or procure to be printed,
reprinted, or imported for sale, or shall publish, sell, or
otherwise dispose of, or cause or procure to be published, sold,
or otherwise disposed of, any copy or copies of any historical
print or prints, or any print or prints of any portrait, conversation, landscape, or architecture, map, chart, or plan,
or any other print or prints whatsoever, which hath or
have been or shall be engraved, etched, drawn, or designed in any part of Great Britain, without the express
consent of the proprietor or proprietors thereof first had
and obtained in writing, signed by him, her, or them
respectively, with his, her, or their own hands in the presence of, and attested by, two or more credible witnesses,
then every such proprietor or proprietors shall, and may,
by and in a special action upon the case, to be brought
against the person or persons so offending, recover such
damages as a jury on the trial of such action, or on the
execution of a writ of inquiry thereon, shall give or assess,
together with double costs of suit.*

* Double cost abolished by 24 and 25 Vic., c. 101.

54 George III., c. 56.

An Act to amend and render more effectual an Act of His present Majesty, for encouraging the Art of making new Models and Casts of Busts, and other Things therein mentioned; and for giving further Encouragment to such Arts.

[18th May, 1814.]

WHEREAS, by an Act, passed in the thirty-eighth year of the reign of His present Majesty, intituled "An Act for encouraging the Art of Making new Models and Casts of Busts, and other Things therein mentioned," the sole right and property thereof were vested in the original proprietors for a time therein specified ; And whereas the provisions of the said Act having been found ineffectual for the purposes thereby intended, it is expedient to amend the same, and to make other provisions and regulations for the encouragement of artists, and to secure to them the profits of and in their works, and for the advancement of the said Arts: May it therefore please your Majesty that it may be enacted, and be it enacted by the King's most excellent Majesty, by and with the advice and consent of the Lords spiritual and temporal, and Commons in this present Parliament assembled, and by the authority of the same, That from and after the passing of this Act, every person or persons who shall make or cause to be made, any new and original sculpture, or model, or copy, or cast of the human figure, or human figures, or of any bust or busts, or of any part or parts of the human figure, clothed in drapery or otherwise, or of any animal or animals, or of any part or parts of any animal combined with the human figure or otherwise, or of any subject being matter of invention in sculpture, or of any alto or basso-relievo representing any of the matters or things hereinbefore mentioned, or any cast from nature of the human figure, or of any part or parts of the human figure, or of any cast from nature of any animal, or of any part or parts of any animal, or of any such subject containing or representing any of the matters and things hereinbefore mentioned, whether separate or combined, shall have the sole right and property of all and in every such new and original sculpture, model, copy, and cast of the human figure or human figures, and of all and in every such bust or busts, and of all and in every such part or parts of the human figure, clothed in drapery or otherwise, and of all and in every such new and original sculpture, model, copy, and cast, representing any animal or animals, and of all and in every such work representing any part or parts of any animal combined wtth the human figure or otherwise, and of all and in every such new and original sculpture, model, copy, and cast of any subject, being matter of invention in sculpture, and of all and in every such new and original sculpture, model, copy, and cast in alto or basso-relievo, representing any of the matters or things hereinbefore mentioned, and of any such cast from nature, for the term of fourteen years from first putting forth or publishing the same: Provided, in all and in every case, the proprietor or proprietors do cause his, her, or their name or names, with the date, to be put on all and every such new and original sculpture, model, copy, or cast, and on every such cast from nature, before the same shall be put forth or published.

II. And be it further enacted, That the sole right and property of all works, which have been put forth or published under the protection of the said recited Act, shall be extended, continued to, and vested in, the respective proprietors thereof for the term of fourteen years, to commence from the date when such last-mentioned works respectively were put forth and published.

III. And be it further enacted, that if any person or persons shall, within such term of fourteen years, make or import, or cause to be made or imported, or exposed to sale, or otherwise disposed of, any pirated copy or pirated

cast of any such new and original sculpture, or model, or
copy, or cast of the human figure or human figures, or of
any such bust or busts, or of any such part or parts
of the human figure, clothed in drapery or otherwise, or of any such work of any animal or animals,
or of any such part or parts of any animal or animals
combined with the human figure or otherwise, or of any
such subject being matter of invention in sculpture, or of
any such alto or basso-relievo representing any of the matters
or things hereinbefore mentioned, or of any such casts from
nature as aforesaid, whether such pirated copy or pirated
cast be produced by moulding or copying from, or imitating in any way, any of the matters or things put forth or
published under the protection of this Act, or of
any works which have been put forth or published
under the protection of the said recited Act, the
right and property whereof is and are secured, extended,
and protected by this Act in any of the cases as aforesaid,
to the detriment, damage, or loss of the original or respective proprietor or proprietors of any such works so pirated ;
then in all such cases the said proprietor or proprietors, or
their assignee or assignees, shall, and may, by and in a
special action upon the case to be brought against the
person or persons so offending, receive such damages as a
jury on a trial of such action shall give or assess,
together with double cost of suit.

IV. Provided, nevertheless, That no person or persons
who shall or may hereafter purchase the right or property
of any new and original sculpture or model, or copy or
cast, or of any cast from nature, or of any of the matters
and things published under, or protected by virtue of this
Act, of the proprietor or proprietors, expressed in a deed in
writing signed by him, her, or them respectively, with his,
her, or their own hand or hands, in the presence of, and
attested by, two or more credible witnesses, shall be subject to any action for copying, or casting, or vending the
same, anything contained in this Act to the contrary
notwithstanding.

V. Provided always, and be it further enacted, That all actions to be brought as aforesaid, against any person or persons for any offence committed against this Act, shall be commenced within six calendar months next after the discovery of every such offence, and not afterwards.

VI. Provided always, and be it further enacted, That from and immediately after the expiration of the said term of fourteen years, the sole right of making and disposing of such new and original sculpture, or model, or copy, or cast of any of the matters or things hereinbefore mentioned, shall return to the person or persons who originally made, or caused to be made the same, if he or they shall be then living, for the further term of fourteen years, excepting in the case or cases where such person or persons shall by sale or otherwise, have divested himself, herself, or themselves, of such right of making or disposing of any new and original sculpture, or model, or copy, or cast of any of the matters or things hereinbefore mentioned, previous to the passing of this Act.

5 & 6 Vict., c. 45, ss. 11, 12 & 14.

XI. And be it enacted, That a book of registry, wherein may be registered, as hereinafter enacted, the proprietorship in the copyright of books, and assignments thereof, and in dramatic and musical pieces, whether in manuscript or otherwise, and licenses affecting such copyright, shall be kept at the Hall of the Stationers' Company by the officer appointed by the said Company for the purposes of this Act, and shall at all convenient times be open to the inspection of any person, on payment of one shilling for every entry which shall be searched for or inspected in the said book ; and that such officer shall, whenever thereunto reasonably required, give a copy of any entry in such book, certified under his hand, and impressed with the stamp of the said Company, to be provided by them for that purpose, and which they are hereby required to provide, to any person requiring the same, on payment to him of the sum

of five shillings; and such copies so certified and impressed shall be received in evidence in all courts, and in
all summary proceedings, and shall be *primâ facie* proof
of the proprietorship or assignment of copyright or
license as therein expressed, but subject to be rebutted by
other evidence, and, in the case of dramatic and musical
pieces, shall be *primâ facie* proof of the right of representation or performance, subject to be rebutted as aforesaid.

XII. And be it enacted, That if any person shall wilfully make, or cause to be made, any false entry in the
registry book of the Stationers' Company, or shall wilfully
produce or cause to be tendered in evidence any paper
falsely purporting to be a copy of any entry in the said
book, he shall be guilty of an indictable misdemeanor, and
shall be punished accordingly.

XIV. And be it enacted, That if any person shall deem
himself aggrieved by any entry made under colour of this
Act in the said book of registry, it shall be lawful for
such person to apply by motion to the Court of Queen's
Bench, Court of Common Pleas, or Court of Exchequer,
in term time, or to apply by summons to any judge of
either such Courts in vacation, for an order that such
entry may be expunged or varied ; and that upon any
such application by motion or summons to either of the
said Courts, or to a Judge as aforesaid, such Court or
Judge shall make such order for expunging, varying, or
confirming such entry, either with or without costs, as to
such Court or Judge shall seem just; and the officer appointed by the Stationers' Company for the purposes of
this Act shall, on the production to him of any such
order for expunging or varying any such entry, expunge
or vary the same according to the requisitions of such
order.

13 & 14 Vict., c. 104, ss. 6 & 7.

An Act to extend and amend the Acts relating to the Copy-right of Designs.

[14th August, 1850.]

VI. That the Registrar of Designs, upon application by or on behalf of the proprietor of any sculpture, model, copy, or cast within the protection of the Sculpture Copy-right Acts, and upon being furnished with such copy, drawing, print, or description, in writing or in print, as in the judgment of the said registrar shall be sufficient to identify the particular sculpture, model, copy, or cast, in respect of which registration is desired, and the name of the person claiming to be proprietor, together with his place of abode, or business, or other place of address, or the name, style, or title of the firm under which he may be trading, shall register such sculpture, model, copy, or cast in such manner and form as shall from time to time be prescribed or approved by the Board of Trade for the whole or any part of the term during which copyright in such sculpture, model, copy, or cast may or shall exist under the Sculpture Copyright Acts ; and whenever any such registration shall be made, the said registrar shall certify under his hand and seal of office, in such form as the said board shall direct or approve, the fact of such registration, and the date of the same, and the name of the registered proprietor, or the style or title of the firm under which such proprietor may be trading, together with his place of abode or business or other place of address.

VII. That if any person shall, during the continuance of the copyright in any sculpture, model, copy, or cast which shall have been so registered as aforesaid, make, import, or cause to be made, imported, exposed for sale, or otherwise disposed of, any pirated copy or pirated cast of any such sculpture, model, copy or cast, in such manner and under such circumstances as would entitle the proprietor to a special action on the case under the Sculpture Copyright Acts, the person so offending shall forfeit for every such offence a sum not less than five pounds, and not exceeding thirty pounds, to the proprietor of the sculpture, model, copy or cast whereof the copyright shall have been infringed; and for the recovery of such penalty the proprietor of the sculpture, model, copy or cast which shall have been so pirated, shall have and be entitled to the same remedies as are provided for the recovery of penalties incurred under the Designs Act, 1842. Provided always, that the proprietor of any sculpture, model, copy or cast which shall be registered under this Act shall not be entitled to the benefit of this Act, unless every copy or cast of such sculpture, model, copy or cast which shall be published by him after such registration shall be marked with the word " registered," and with the date of registration.

25 & 26 Vict., c. 68.

An Act for Amending the Law relating to Copyright in Works of the Fine Arts, and for Repressing the Commission of Fraud in the Production and Sale of such Works.

[29th July, 1862.]

WHEREAS by law, as now established, the authors of paintings, drawings and photographs, have no copyright in such their works, and it is expedient that the law should in that respect be amended : Be it therefore enacted by the Queen's most excellent Majesty, by and with the advice and consent of the Lords spiritual and temporal, and Commons in this present Parliament assembled, and by the authority of the same, as follows :

I. The author, being a British subject or resident within the dominions of the Crown, of every original painting, drawing and photograph, which shall be or shall have been made either in the British dominions or elsewhere, and which shall not have been sold or disposed of before the commencement of this Act, and his assigns, shall have the sole and exclusive right of copying, engraving, reproducing, and multiplying such painting or drawing, and the design thereof, or such photograph, and the negative thereof, by any means and of any size, for the term of the natural life of such author, and seven years after his death; provided that when any painting or drawing, or the negative of any photograph, shall for the first time after the passing of this Act be sold or disposed of, or shall be made or executed for or on behalf of any other person for a good or a valuable consideration, the person so selling or disposing of, or making or executing the same, shall not retain the copyright thereof, unless it be expressly reserved to him by agreement in writing, signed, at or before the time of such sale or disposition, by the vendee or assignee of such painting or drawing, or of such negative of a photograph, or by the person for and on whose behalf the same shall be so made or executed, but the copyright shall belong to the vendee or assignee of such painting or drawing, or of such negative of a photograph, or to the person for or on whose behalf the same shall have been made or executed; nor shall the vendee or assignee thereof be entitled to any such copyright, unless, at or before the time of such sale or disposition, an agreement in writing, signed by the person so selling or disposing of the same, or by his agent duly authorised, shall have been made to that effect.

II. Nothing herein contained shall prejudice the right of any person to copy or use any work in which there shall be no copyright, or to represent any scene or object, notwithstanding that there may be copyright in some representation of such scene or object.

III. All copyright under this Act shall be deemed personal or moveable estate, and shall be assignable at law, and every assignment thereof, and every licence to use or

copy by any means or process the design or work which
shall be the subject of such copyright, shall be made by
some note or memorandum in writing, to be signed by the
proprietor of the copyright, or by his agent appointed for
that purpose in writing.

IV. There shall be kept at the Hall of the Stationers'
Company, by the officer appointed by the said Company
for the purposes of the Act passed in the sixth year of
the reign of Her present Majesty, intituled, " An Act to
Amend the Law of Copyright," a book or books entitled,
"The Register of Proprietors of Copyright in Paintings,
Drawings and Photographs," wherein shall be entered a
memorandum of every copyright to which any person
shall be entitled under this Act, and also of every subsequent assignment of any such copyright; and such
memorandum shall contain a statement of the date of such
agreement or assignment, and of the names of the parties
thereto, and of the name and place of abode of the person
in whom such copyright shall be vested by virtue thereof,
and of the name and place of abode of the author of
the work in which there shall be such copyright, together
with a short description of the nature and subject of such
work, and in addition thereto, if the person registering
shall so desire, a sketch, outline, or photograph of the said
work ; and no proprietor of any such copyright shall be
entitled to the benefit of this Act until such registration,
and no action shall be sustainable, nor any penalty be
recoverable in respect of anything done before registration.

V. The several enactments in the said Act of the sixth
year of Her present Majesty contained, with relation to
keeping the register book thereby required, and the inspection thereof, the searches therein, and the delivery of certified and stamped copies thereof, the reception of such
copies in evidence, the making of false entries in the said
book, and the production in evidence of papers falsely purporting to be copies of entries in the said book, the application to the Courts and Judges by persons aggrieved by entries in the said book, and the expunging and varying such

entries, shall apply to the book or books to be kept by virtue of this Act, and to the entries and assignments of copyright and proprietorship therein under this Act, in such and the same manner as if such enactments were here expressly enacted in relation thereto, save and except that the forms of entry prescribed by the said Act of the sixth year of Her present Majesty may be varied to meet the cir-·cumstances of the case, and that the sum to be demanded by the officer of the said Company of Stationers for making any entry reouired by this Act shall be one shilling ·only.

VI. If the author of any painting, drawing, or photo-graph in which there shall be subsisting copyright, after having sold or disposed of such copyright, or if any other person, not being the proprietor for the time being of copy-right in any painting, drawing or photograph, shall, without the consent of such proprietor, repeat, copy, colourably imi-tate, or otherwise multiply for sale, hire, exhibition or dis-·tribution, or cause or procure to be repeated, copied, colourably imitated, or otherwise multiplied for sale, hire, exhibition, or distribution any such work or the design thereof, or knowing that any such repetition, copy, or ·other imitation has been unlawfully made, shall import into any part of the United Kingdom, or sell, publish, let to hire, exhibit, or distribute, or offer for sale, hire, exhibi-tion, or distribution, or cause or procure to be imported, sold, published, let to hire, distributed, or offered for sale, hire, ex-hibition, or distribution, any repetition, copy, or imitation of the said work, or of the design thereof, made without such consent aforesaid, such person for every such offence shall forfeit to the proprietor of the copyright for the time being a sum not exceeding ten pounds ; and all such repetitions, copies, and imitations made without such consent as afore-said, and all negatives of photographs made for the purpose of obtaining such copies, shall be forfeited to the proprietor of the copyright.

VII. No person shall do, or cause to be done, any or either of the following acts : that is to say,

H

First, no person shall fraudulently sign or otherwise affix, nor fraudulently cause to be signed or otherwise affixed, to or upon any painting, drawing, or photograph, or the negative thereof, any name, initials, or monogram :

Secondly, no person shall fraudulently sell, publish, exhibit, or dispose of, or offer for sale, exhibition, or distribution, any painting, drawing or photograph, or negative of a photograph, having thereon the name, initials, or monogram of a person who did not execute or make such work :

Thirdly, no person shall fraudulently utter, dispose of, or put off, or cause to be uttered or disposed of, any copy or colourable imitation of any painting, drawing, or photograph, or negative of a photograph, whether there shall be subsisting copyright therein or not, as have been made or executed by the author or maker of the original work from which such copy or imitation shall have been taken :

Fourthly, where the author or maker of any painting, drawing, or photograph, or negative of a photograph, made either before or after the passing of this Act, shall have sold or otherwise parted with the possession of such work, if any alteration shall afterwards be made therein by any other person, by addition or otherwise, no person shall be at liberty, during the life of the author or maker of such work, without his consent, to make or knowingly to sell, or publish, or offer for sale, such work or any copies of such work so altered as aforesaid, or of any part thereof, as or for the unaltered work of such author or maker :

Every offender under this section shall, upon conviction, forfeit to the person aggrieved a sum not exceeding ten pounds, or not exceeding double the full price, if any, at which all such copies, engravings, imitations, or altered works shall have been sold or offered for sale ; and all such copies, engravings, imitations, or altered works shall be forfeited to the person, or the assigns or legal representatives of the person, whose name, initials, or monogram shall shall be so fraudulently signed or affixed thereto, or to whom such spurious or altered work shall be so fraudulently or falsely prescribed as aforesaid : Provided always, that the penalties imposed by this section shall not be incurred unless the person whose name, initials, or monogram shall be so fraudulently signed or affixed, or to whom such spurious or altered work shall be so fraudulently or falsely ascribed as aforesaid, shall have been living at or within twenty years next before the time when the offence may have been committed.

VIII. All pecuniary penalties which shall be incurred, and all such unlawful copies, imitations, and all other effects and things as shall have been forfeited by offenders, pursuant to this Act, and pursuant to any Act for the protection of copyright engravings, may be recovered by the person hereinbefore, and in any such Act as aforesaid empowered to recover the same respectively, and hereinafter called the complainant or complainer, as follows :

In England and Ireland, either by action against the party offending or by summary proceedings before any two justices having jurisdiction where the party offending resides :

In Scotland, by action before the Court of Sessions in ordinary form, or by summary action before the Sheriff of the County where the offence may be committed or the offender resides, who, upon proof of the offence or offences, either by confession of the party offending, or by the oath or affirmation of one or more credible witnesses, shall convict the offender, and find him liable to the penalty or penalties aforesaid, as also in expenses; and it shall be lawful for the Sheriff, in pronouncing such judgment for the penalty or penalties and costs, to insert in such judgment a warrant, in the event of such penalty or penalties and costs not being paid, to levy and recover the amount of the same by poinding: Provided always, that it shall be lawful to the Sheriff, in the event of his dismissing the action and assoilzieing the defender, to find the complainer liable in expenses, and any judgment so to be pronounced by the Sheriff in such summary application shall be final and conclusive, and not subject to review by advocation, suspension, reduction or otherwise.

IX. In any action in any of Her Majesty's Superior Courts of Record at Westminster and in Dublin, for the infringement of any such copyright as aforesaid, it shall be lawful for the Court in which such action is pending, if the Court be then sitting, or if the Court be not sitting then for a Judge of such Court, on the application of the plaintiff or defendant respectively, to make such order for an injunction, inspection, or account, and to give such direction respecting such action, injunction, inspection and account, and the procedings therein respectively, as to such Court or Judge may seem fit.

X.—All repetitions, copies, or imitations of paintings, drawings or photographs, wherein or in the design whereof there shall be subsisting copyright under this Act, and all repetitions, copies and imitations of the designs of any such painting or drawing, or of the negative of any such photograph which, contrary to the provisions of this Act, shall have been made in any foreign State, or in any part of the British Dominions, are hereby absolutely prohibited to be imported into any part of the United Kingdom, except by or with the consent of the proprietor of the copyright thereof, or his agent authorised in writing; and if the proprietor of any such copyright, or his agent, shall declare that any goods imported are repetitions, copies, or imitations of any such painting, drawing, or photograph, or of the negative of any such photograph, and so prohibited as aforesaid, then such goods may be detained by the officers of Her Majesty's Customs.

XI.—If the author of any painting, drawing or photograph in which there shall be subsisting copyright after having sold or otherwise disposed of such copyright, or if any other person, not being the proprietor for the time being of such copyright, shall, without the consent of such proprietor, repeat, copy, colourably imitate or otherwise multiply, or cause or procure to be repeated, copied, colourably imitated or otherwise multiplied, for sale, hire, exhibition, or distribution, any such work or the design thereof, or the negative of any such photograph, or shall import or cause to be imported into any part of the United Kingdom, or sell, publish, let to hire, exhibit, or distribute or offer for sale, hire, exhibition or distribution, or cause or procure to be sold, published, let to hire, exhibited or distributed, or offered for sale, hire, exhibition or distribution any repetition, copy or imitation of such work, or the design thereof, or the negative of any such photograph made without such consent as aforesaid, then every such proprietor, in addition to the remedies hereby given for the recovery of any such penalties, and forfeiture of any such things as aforesaid, may recover damages by and in a special action on the case, to be brought against the person so offending, and may in such action recover and enforce the delivery to him of all unlawful repetitions, copies, and imitations, and negatives of photographs, or may recover damages for the retention or conversion thereof: Provided that nothing herein contained, nor any proceeding, conviction or judgment, for any act hereby forbidden, shall affect any remedy which any person aggrieved by such Act may be entitled to, either at law or in equity.

XII. This Act may be considered as including the provisions of the Act passed in the Session of Parliament held in the seventh and eighth year of Her present Majesty, intituled, " An Act to Amend the Law relating to International Copyright," in the same manner as if such provisions were part of this Act.

FORMS.

FORM I.

Form for the Entire Reservation of Copyright by the Author, whether his work has been Commissioned or not.

PAINTINGS.   DRAWINGS.   PHOTOGRAPHS.

IT IS HEREBY AGREED between

Artist,

residing at   in the United

Kingdom, and the undersigned

of

that the Copyright of the Painting entitled

representing

made by the said

and now sold for the first time to me, is reserved to the

said

Signed

Dated

FORM 2.

Form of Sale of Copyright by Artist.

PAINTINGS.   DRAWINGS.   PHOTOGRAPHS.

IT IS HEREBY AGREED between the under-signed,

residing at   in the United Kingdom, Artist, and   of

that in consideration of the Sum of £

over and above the Price of the Work hereinafter described,

paid by the said   to the said   the said   is entitled to the

Copyright in the Painting made by the said

entitled

and representing

now first sold or disposed of to the said

[If any additional terms be agreed upon, add them here, *e.g.*, that the Artist be at liberty to sell replicas, studies, or sketches.]

Signed

Dated

FORM 3.

Form of Assignment of Copyright by the person who has acquired it from the Artist.

PAINTINGS.   DRAWINGS.   PHOTOGRAPHS.

[*Address*]

I,   of

being the pro-
prietor of the Copyright for all purposes in a painting
made by   Artist, of
entitled   and representing
hereby in consideration of £
sell and assign all such my Copyright.

[If any additional terms be agreed upon, add them here.]

Signed

To [*name of assignee*]
of

Dated

Form 4.

For partial reservation of Copyright by the Author in case of Commissioned work.

PAINTINGS.   DRAWINGS.   PHOTOGRAPHS.

[*Address and Date.*]

As at my request you have made a painting for me at the price of £   entitled
and representing]   I admit that at, or prior to, the time of the same being delivered to me, I agreed with you that all Copyright for the purposes of making (*say an etching*) should be your property, and that you should be entitled to sell, or otherwise dispose of, all sketches and studies, made or executed in connection with the said work.

Signed

To   Artist,

of

FORM 5.

License by Proprietor of Copyright.

PAINTINGS.   DRAWINGS.   PHOTOGRAPHS. SCULPTURES.

To   of

I HEREBY, in consideration of £

paid to me by you, grant and assign to you for the purpose of producing a

of the size of   and for no other
purpose whatever, this exclusive license to copy the Painting *(or as the case may be)* entitled

representing

made by me [here add any other terms that may be agreed
upon, *e.g.*, " And I undertake not to reproduce the work
in a similar manner."]

Signed

Address

Dated

FORM 6.

Form of Sale and Assignment of License by Licensee from Owner of Copyright.

PAINTINGS. DRAWINGS. PHOTOGRAPHS. SCULPTURES.

[Address and Date.]

I, being the proprietor of a License to Copy a Painting, [or as the case may be ; here copy the words of the License in every particular] in consideration of the sum of £ hereby sell and assign such License to you. [If any additional terms be agreed upon, add them here.]

Signed

To

[Address]

FORM 7.

Form of Assignment of Copyright in Etchings and Engravings.

ETCHINGS. ENGRAVINGS. LITHOGRAPHS.

To .   of

   I,   being the

Proprietor of the Copyright in my

entitled

hereby, in consideration of the Sum of £

assign the said Copyright in the said

to you.

   Signed by me this   day of   18

In the presence of Two Witnesses.

                    1.

                    2.

      N.B.—No registration is necessary.

FORM 8.

*Form of Appointment of Agent for the Sale of Copyright,
or to give a License to Copy.*

PAINTINGS.   DRAWINGS.   PHOTOGRAPHS.

[*Address*]

Date

I HEREBY APPOINT you my Agent to Sell the
Copyright in, or to give a License to engrave, a Painting
made by   entitled
and representing

[*Signature of proprietor of copyright.*]

To

[*Name and Address of Agent*]

Memorandum for Registration under Copyright (Works of Art) Act.

Price of Form, 1d.   Fee, 1s.

TO THE REGISTERING OFFICER APPOINTED BY THE STATIONERS' COMPANY.

I,   of

do hereby certify, That I am entitled to the Copyright in the undermentioned Work ; and I hereby require a Memorandum of such Copyright [*or* the Assignment of such Copyright,] to be entered in the Register of Proprietors of Copyright in Paintings, Drawings, and Photographs, kept at Stationers' Hall, according to the particulars underwritten.

(Every particular given must be clearly written.)

Description of Work.	Date of Agreement or Assignment. *	Names of Parties to Agreement.*	Name and Place of Abode of Proprietor of Copyright.	Name and Place of Abode of Author of Work.

Dated this   day of   , 188—.

(Signed)

N.B.—Office Hours, 10 to 4 ; *Saturdays* 10 to 2.

* If the work be commissioned work, and the commissioner is still the owner of the copyright, he should leave these spaces blank.

La Forme pour requérir l'Enregistrement de Propriété à Stationers' Hall, London.

A MONSIEUR LE REGISTRAIRE NOMMÉ PAR LA CORPORA-
TION DES LIBRAIRES.

Moi,   de
je certifie par ceci, que je suis le Propriétaire du Droit
d'Auteur d'um Livre, intitulé   et je
vous require par ceci d'inscrire sur le Livre d'Enregistrement de la Corporation des Libraires ma Propriété du tel
Droit d'Auteur selon les détails ci dessous ecrits.

Le Titre du Livre.	Le Nom et La De-meure d'Auteur on du Compositeur.	Le Nom et la De-meure de Proprie-taire du Droit d'Auteur.	L'Epoque et la Lieu de la première Publi cation.

Daté ce   jour de   , 18—.

Témoin   (Signé)

(N.B.—Il faut que tous le détails soient ecrits très clare-
ment.)

Form of original entry under International Copyright Act.

This Form is, at present, used for every work, whether
Book, Print, Piece of Sculpture; whether, French, German, &c., &c.

The foregoing Form should be altered to suit the requirements of the International Copyright Acts in the case of works of art, the particulars required being, in the case of registry of a

Print.	The Title.	Name and Place of Abode of Master, Designer, or Engraver.	Name and Address of Proprietor of Copyright.	Date of First Publication in Foreign Country.
Sculpture.	Descriptive Title.	Ditto of Sculptor.	Ditto.	Ditto.
Painting, Drawing, or Photograph.	Short description of nature and subject of Work, and, if desired by the person registering, a sketch, outline, or photograph.	Ditto of Author.	Ditto.	Ditto.

N.B.—In the case of a print, a copy of such print upon the best paper upon which the largest number of impressions shall have been printed for sale must be deposited.

Form of Assignment of Copyright in Sculpture.

This indenture, &c., between A. (assignor) of, &c., of the one part, and P. (purchaser) of, &c., of the other part. Whereas the said (A) has executed a (statue), entitled, &c., and representing, &c., and hath contracted with the said (P) for the absolute sale of the copyright of the said work for the sum of £—, Now this indenture witnesseth, That in consideration of the sum of £— to the said (A), well and truly paid by the said (P), he the said (A) doth grant, assign, and set over, All that the said (statue) and the whole, entire, and exclusive copyright, and all and singular the right, title, &c., of him the said (A) of and in and to the same. To Have and to Hold the said (statue) and copyright, and all the profit and advantage that shall and may arise from the reproduction and vending of the same unto the said (P), his executors, administrators, and assigns, as fully and beneficially, and for such time and respective times as the said (A) can or may assign the same. In witness, &c.

LAW AMENDMENT SOCIETY,

1, ADAM STREET, ADELPHI, W.C.

REPORT ON COPYRIGHT,

Adopted by the Council, February 17th, 1881.

Your Sub-Committee have met five times, and have been favoured with the assistance of Mr. Basil Field, representing the interests of artists, and of Messrs. Bolton and Mote, representing those of dramatic authors. The result of their labours has been the adoption of the following heads for a Bill, which in the matter of artistic copyright mainly agree with a memorial presented to Her Majesty's Government by the Royal Academy on the subject of the recommendations of the Royal Commissioners relating to artistic copyright, and in the rest of the subject mainly agree with the Report of the Royal Commissioners, except that with regard to the duration of copyright, other than artistic, your Sub-Committee have of course followed the direction given to them :—

1. That registration of copyright in works of all classes published in the United Kingdom, and in dramatic or musical works first performed in the United Kingdom though not published (but not in paintings, drawings, or sculpture, since there is nothing in them analogous to publication), should be compulsory; that is to say, as recommended by the Royal Commissioners, that a copyright owner should not be entitled to take or maintain any proceedings, or to recover any penalty in respect of his

copyright until he has registered, and that he should in no case be able to proceed after registration for acts of piracy preceding it.

2. That if owners of copyrights in paintings, drawings, or sculpture, should desire to register their copyrights, for the purpose of evidencing their title or otherwise, they should have power to do so.

3. That to ensure the system of compulsory registration being properly managed and complete, and having regard to the general importance of the subject and the magnitude of the interests involved, it is desirable that registration should be effected at a Government Office, to be established and maintained for that purpose in the manner recommended by the Royal Commissioners, and that a register should no longer be maintained at Stationers' Hall.

4. That in the case of books, photographs, engravings, prints, or similar works, copyright should mean the exclusive right of multiplying copies of the work protected, including, in the case of engravings, prints or similar works, the exclusive right of multiplying copies of them by photography or any other kind of art. That in the case of lectures, if printed and published, copyright should mean the exclusive right both of multiplying copies of the lectures and of re-delivering them. That in the case of musical or dramatic works, copyright should mean the exclusive right of multiplying copies of the works protected, and that the exclusive right of performing them should be originally annexed thereto, so that the two may be secured by one and the same registration; but that after such registration the copyright and performing right in musical and dramatic works should be assignable separately.

5. That the term of copyright in all the cases defined in Clause 4, and also the term of the performing right in musical and dramatic works, should, in accordance with your Resolution, be fifty years from the date of registration.

6. That in the case of paintings, drawings or sculpture,

copyright should mean the exclusive right of multiplying copies of the design of the work protected, whether in the same or any other material or kind of art, as by painting, drawing, modelling, photography, engraving or otherwise, and whether of the same or any other dimensions.

7.   That in the case of paintings, drawings or sculpture, the term of copyright should be the life of the artist and thirty years after his death.

8.   That on the sale of a painting, drawing, or piece of sculpture, or when such a work is executed on commission, the copyright in it should remain with the artist in the absence of a written agreement to the contrary ; but that the purchaser or other owner should have an equal power with the artist or other owner of the copyright to prevent third parties copying its design in any manner which would be an infringement of such copyright.   If the work, or the chief part of it, be the likeness of the purchaser, or of any person whose likeness was stipulated in the commission for the work, the consent of the purchaser or other owner of the work should be necessary for the reproduction of its design in any manner by the artist or other owner of the copyright.   That the purchaser or other owner of a painting or drawing should be protected against replicas.*

9.   That the present law by which, in the case of articles in magazines, reviews, or other collective works except encyclopædias, written and paid for on the terms that the copyright shall belong to the proprietor of the collective work, a right of separate publication reverts to the author after twenty-eight years, should be modified, three years being substituted for twenty-eight; and that during the three years the author of an article as well as the proprietor of the collective work should have power to take proceedings in order to repress piracy.

---

* The Bill will also contain a clause empowering the artist who has sold his copyright in a work to sell *bonâ fide* sketches and studies used in its composition, or to use them again, provided that he do not repeat the design of the work.

10.   That the present law as to presentation of books to the British Museum and other libraries should remain un-altered.

11.   That in the case of British subjects copyright under the Act to be passed should extend to all the British dominions, and should be enjoyed in respect of paintings, drawings or pieces of sculpture wherever made, and in respect of works of all other classes first published or per-formed in any part of the British dominions, and registered either in the United Kingdom or in such other part of the British dominions as they were respectively first published or performed in, if registration should be required for copy-right by the law of that part of the British dominions in which they were first published or performed.

12.   That aliens, wherever resident, should be entitled to copyright in paintings, drawings, and sculpture, if they bring their works into the British dominions in order to retain or sell them there; and to copyright in works of all other classes, on satisfying the conditions expressed in Clause 11.

13.   That a British author, who first publishes his work out of the British dominions, or whose play or musical composition is first performed out of those dominions, should not be prevented thereby from obtaining copyright in those dominions by subsequent publication or perform-ance therein, together with registration where necessary as aforesaid, provided such conditions be satisfied within three years from the first publication or performance abroad.

14.   That the power to search houses for piratical copies and photographs of pictures, which was proposed to be given in the Copyright Bill of 1869, should be conferred.*

15.   That the power to seize piratical copies and photo-graphs of pictures being hawked about for sale, which was proposed to be given in the Copyright Bill of 1869, should be conferred.*

* This power will extend to the case of piratical copies and photographs of works of sculpture, engraving, and photography, as well as of pictures.

16.   That with regard to the colonial question, the recommendations contained in paragraphs 182-216 of the report of the Royal Commissioners should be carried into effect.*

17.   That the licensed colonial reprints referred to in paragraph 217 of the Royal Commissioners' report should be admitted without restriction into all parts of the British dominions.

18.   That with regard to copyright in foreign works under the International Copyright Acts, the necessity for registration in this country, and for the deposit of a copy of the foreign work, imposed by the Statute 7 and 8 Vict., c. 12, should be abolished, as recommended by the Royal Commissioners.

19.   That with regard to the right of translation of foreign books and plays, the necessity for registration and deposit of a copy of the work, as well as that for publication and registration of translations, whether partial or complete, imposed by the Statute 15 and 16 Vic., c. 12, should be abolished, as recommended by the Royal Commissioners.

20.   That in lieu of the present law, there should be reserved to authors and playwrights of any State with which there exists a copyright treaty a general right, during three years, of translating their books and plays, and of adapting their plays for the English stage ; and that if the author or playwright exercises such right during the three years, he should have a copyright for ten years from the date of registering the translation or adaptation, together with performing right for the same period in the case of the translation or adaptation of a play.

21.   That if the foreign author or playwright does not exercise the right reserved to him under the preceding clause, it should be lawful for anyone to translate or adapt the book or play, and thereby to acquire copyright and performing right for ten years from the date of registering the translation or adaptation.

To prepare a Bill on copyright, embracing the whole

* See *Note* on p. 119.

subject and giving effect to the above heads, would be a work of great labour and expense: and your Sub-Committee . are therefore unable at present to do more than to report the conclusions they have arrived at, and to recommend to the Council of the Society that it should take such steps as may seem advisable with a view to meeting the necessary cost of obtaining legislation. The Bankruptcy Bill of 1859, and the Artizans' Dwellings Bill, are instances in which the Society has defrayed or contributed to the cost of legislation ; and while your Sub-Committee believe that in the present instance large pecuniary support may be found outside, they also think that the occasion is one which would justisfy such a contribution from the funds of the Society as it may be able to afford.

J. WESTLAKE.
J. LEYBOURN GODDARD.
WILLIAM FOOKS.

Note to paragraphs numbered 16 & 17 of Sub-Committee's Report.

As many persons are not in possession of a copy of the Report of the Royal Commission on Copyright, and some are not well acquainted with the "colonial question," it may be well to give the following particulars, which are fuly discussed in paragraphs 182—216 of that Report :—

The Commissioners had previously shown that the present law, which gives copyright throughout the British dominions if a book be published in the United Kingdom, but not outside the colony of publication, if published in a colony, is anomalous and unsatisfactory, and for a remedy had suggested that publication of a book in any part of the British dominions should secure copyright throughout those dominions, but this is not sufficient to meet all the wants of the colonists. It was considered highly desirable that the literature of this country should be placed within easy reach of the colonies, but to effect this the law, it was stated, required amendment. For the sake of profit it is a common practice in this country to publish books of literary merit first at a very high or fancy price, and afterwards, but not for a long time, at cheaper rates, and the consequent difficulty in procuring them at first, when only published at the high price, is met by means of circulating libraries and book clubs. These means, however, are not available in the colonies, so that until the cheap editions of these books are published, which generally happens after the sale of the expensive editions has ceased, and when the freshness of the work is worn off, colonists cannot afford to get them, even if they can get them then, and thus they are deprived of the power of getting English books till they have lost their novelty and are frequently of little interest. This was felt to be such a grievance after the Copyright

Act of 1842 was passed, that in 1847 an Act called the Foreign Reprints' Act was passed.   To make the scheme and effect of this Act understood it must be explained that Canada was one of the colonies in which the hardship was principally felt, and was also a place in which there seemed to be a remedy at hand.   The Americans, who always resisted a copyright treaty with us, were in the habit, when a new work of any note or interest was published in this country, of republishing it in a very cheap form for the benefit of their own people.   This they could do at an extremely cheap price, for they paid the author nothing, and labour and materials were easily procured.   The effect of this was that numerous American copies were smuggled, contrary to our Customs' Acts and the Act of 1842, over the border into Canada.   To turn this source of supply to account, and yet to get the author some remuneration for the injury he sustained by having his Canadian market interfered with, was the principal object of the Act of 1847.   This Act applies to all the British colonies, though Canada was specially in view.   It provides that if any colonial legislature should make due provision for securing the rights of British authors in the colony, Her Majesty may issue an Order in Council declaring that all prohibitions by our laws against importing foreign reprints of English copyright books into the colony should be suspended. Certain colonies made provisions for securing remuneration for the authors, which were at the time supposed to be sufficient, and Orders in Council were made, but they proved insufficient.   The Canadian legislature enacted that the American reprints might be imported on payment of a customs' duty of 12½ per cent., which was to be handed over by their Government to the British Government for the author.   Notwithstanding this, American copies were still largely smuggled into the colony, and scarcely anything came to the authors, of which there was great complaint.   The Canadians made a counter-complaint that, although they might import American reprints, they might not re-publish British copyright works themselves, and so get the benefit of the printing and publishing trade, which, under the Foreign Reprints' Act, the Americans had, and they said that it was in consequence of their great extent of frontier, and other local causes, that they could not prevent smuggling.   The Canadians proposed, by way of remedy, that they should be allowed to republish British copyright works under license from the Governor General on paying an excise duty of 12½ per cent. for the benefit of the authors, and they said they could by that arrangement under-sell the Americans, and so effectually check smuggling, and the British author would be sure of the duty.   The plan, however, was not carried out.   It was then suggested that republication should be allowed in Canada under the author's sanction, and copyright granted to the authors in the Dominion; and a question then arose whether copies so published, which would be published cheaper than the English editions, should be admitted without restriction into this country.   Thereupon the Imperial Act, the Canada Copyright Act, 1875, was passed in order to sanction a Dominion Act, enabling authors to republish in Canada, and so obtain copyright there in addition to their other copyright under the Act of 1842.   The Act had been but a short time in operation when the Royal Commission sat, so that few results could be obtained, but it was shown that books would probably be, and in one instance a book was, republished in Canada at a very considerable reduction in price on the English publishing price, and that American editions

would be kept out.   This Act, therefore, seems to be a success, and the
Commissioners proposed not to interfere with it.   The plan adopted in the
Canada Act is not, however, suitable to small colonies, in which it would
not pay to republish a book, and which must rely on importation for a supply
of literature.   The Commissioners, therefore, proposed that a supply should
be secured for the colonies generally at a cheap price, by the introduction of
a licensing system, and by continuing, though with alterations, the provisions of the Foreign Reprints' Act.   As to the latter the Commissioners said
that, having regard to the power contemplated for authors to obtain colonial
copyright by republication in the colonies, and to the licensing system suggested, they thought foreign reprints should not, except with the consent of
the owner of the copyright, be imported into a colony—1st. When the owner
has availed himself of the local copyright law, if any ; 2nd. Where he has republished in the colony, and so provided an adequate supply ; and, 3rd. When
there has been a republication under the licensing system to be established.
These are the recommendations of the Commissioners, which it is intended
to embody in the proposed Bill. An important question, however, arises upon
them, and that is whether the cheap colonial reprints, which it is the object of the scheme to secure for the colonists, should be admitted without
restriction, that is without paying duty, and on the importation of any person,
into the United Kingdom.   It is probable that the result of their free introduction would be to make books cheaper and prevent fancy prices, and
authors and publishers object to their introduction for that reason, but on
the other hand the interest of the public is that books should be cheap so that
the mass of the people should be able to buy and read them.   The majority
of the Commissioners reported in favour of the publishers, but it is proposed
to provide in the Bill for the admission of colonial reprints, which, it is believed, will be of immense service to the public, and will not, in reality, at
all decrease the profits of either the author or publisher, but, on the contrary,
greatly increase them, for, with cheaper prices, sales will be vastly increased
and profits will grow in proportion.   There is, moreover, an argument in
favour of the admission of colonial cheap prints, which is almost conclusive
—Why should the English people be the only members of the British Empire
who are to be prevented by law from obtaining the cheap books which are
available to all other subjects of the State?

THE COPYRIGHT BILL OF 1881.

This Bill bears the names of Mr. Hastings, Mr. Hanbury Tracy, and Sir Gabriel Goldney. Its material provisions, so far as they relate to works of Art, are given below.

A Bill to Amend and Consolidate the Law relating to Copyright.

WHEREAS it is desirable to amend and consolidate the law of copyright in literary, artistic, musical, and dramatic works, with reference both to the British dominions and to foreign states : and whereas the Commissioners lately appointed by Her Majesty to inquire with regard to the laws and regulations relating to home, colonial, and international copyright, have by their report to Her Majesty made various recommendations, which, with certain exceptions, it is expedient to carry into effect :

Be it therefore enacted by the Queen's most Excellent Majesty, by and with the advice and consent of the Lords Spiritual and Temporal, and Commons, in this present Parliament assembled, and by authority of the same, as follows :

1. This Act may be cited as the Copyright Act, 1881.

2. This Act shall extend to the whole of Her Majesty's dominions.

3. This Act shall be proclaimed in every British possession by the Governor thereof as soon as may be after he receives notice of this Act, and shall come into operation in every part of Her Majesty's dominions on the *first day of January, 1882*, except where otherwise specified in this Act with reference to particular provisions thereof, which day is in this Act referred to as the commencement of this Act : Provided that any Act in a British possession may be passed, and any Order in Council or rule may be made, and anything necessary or proper may be done under or for the purpose of this Act at any time after the passing of this Act.

4. This Act shall, unless it be for particular purposes or as to particular parts expressly provided to the contrary, apply to copyright works other than paintings and sculpture first published after, and to paintings and sculpture which shall be or shall have been made, and which shall not have been sold or disposed of before the passing of this Act only, and not to copyrights existing at the commencement, nor to such works published or sold respectively before the commencement of this Act, nor to any copyright to which a person may be entitled under any law of a British possession ; and all expressions in this Act referring to copyright shall, unless the context otherwise requires, be construed as referring to copyright under this Act only, and all rights and remedies to which a person may be entitled under this Act shall be in addition to and not in derogation of any rights and remedies to which he may be entitled in any British possession under the law of that possession.

5. The Acts or parts of Acts specified in the First Schedule to this Act are hereby repealed as from the commencement of this Act, except with relation to copyrights already existing, and works other than paintings and sculpture already published at, and paintings and sculpture sold or disposed of before the commencement of this Act, but the said Acts shall remain in as full force and effect for the purpose of and with relation to such copyrights and works as if this Act had not been passed. And the Acts or parts of Acts specified in the Second Schedule to this Act are hereby repealed as from the commencement of this Act, except with relation to Orders of Her Majesty in Council made under the authority of the said Acts before the commencement of this Act, and any copyrights, or performing, or other rights already acquired or at any future time to be acquired by virtue of such Orders, but the said Acts or parts of Acts specified in the said Second Schedule shall remain in as full force and effect for the purpose of and with relation to all such Orders, and any copyrights and performing, or other rights thereunder, as if this Act had not been passed.

6. In this Act the following expressions shall, unless the context otherwise requires, have the following meaning :

" Assigns " or " assignees " shall include persons, however remote from the author or producer of a work, in whom the interest of such author or producer in such work or in the copyright therein as the context may imply shall be vested, whether acquired by sale, gift, bequest, operation of law, or otherwise :

"Book" shall mean any volume, part or division of a volume, pamphlet, newspaper, or sheet of letterpress, and any musical composition, print, photograph, or other work published in and forming part of a volume shall be deemed and taken to be a part of the book in which it is published. "Book" shall also include any collection of such works published together so as to form a volume :

"British dominions" shall mean all parts of Her Majesty's dominions, including the United Kingdom :

"British possessions" shall mean any part of Her Majesty's dominions, exclusive of the United Kingdom as defined in this Act, and all places which are under one legislature shall be deemed for the purpose of this Act to constitute one British possession :

"Collective work" shall mean a book which consists of various articles, essays, poems, musical compositions, prints, photographs, or other works written, composed, engraved, made, photographed, or produced by different persons, and published together as one book :

"Commission," when used with reference to the execution of a photograph, shall mean an order for the taking of the negative by a person to whom the work is to belong for valuable consideration :

"Copy," in the case of a photograph, shall mean any repetition or other multiplication thereof, or of the negative thereof, and in the case of a painting, print, or work of sculpture, shall mean any repetition, colourable imitation, or other multiplication of the work, either in whole or in part, or of the design thereof, and of any size, and either in the same form or material in which any such work exists, or any other, and whether produced by the same or any other kind of art than that by which the original work was produced :

"Copyright" shall mean and include,—

In the case of books, the exclusive right of multiplying copies of a book, or any part thereof, by any means or process, and in any size or shape :

In the case of paintings, sculpture, and prints, the exclusive right of multiplying copies of a work in whole or in part, or of the design thereof; and in the case of photographs, the exclusive right of multiplying copies of the same or of the negative thereof, in whole or in part, of any size, and either in the same form or material or by the same kind of art in which any such works respectively exist, or any other,

"Design" shall mean the expression or representation in any form of art of an artist's conception or idea:

"To engrave" shall mean to make, work on, or prepare any plate of steel, copper, zinc, or other material, block of wood or stone, for the purpose of obtaining copies of a painting or print by impression or otherwise, and shall include the act of making copies, prints, or impressions from such plates, blocks, or stones, or by any other process either wholly mechanical, or partly mechanical and partly chemical, whereby prints and impressions are capable of being multiplied:

"Foreign state" shall mean and include every nation or people not under the dominion of Her Majesty:

"Painting" shall mean and include a painting either in oil, distemper, or water colour or colours, and drawing either in crayons, charcoal, pastels, chalk, pencil, ink, or any other material, executed by hand and not by printing impression, or any mechanical or chemical process; and "painter" shall mean any person who has executed a painting as above defined:

"Photograph" shall mean and include the photographic negative, and any positives or copies made therefrom:

"To print," when used with reference to the means of procuring impressions or multiplying copies of a book or other work, shall mean to copy such book or other work, or any part thereof, by any process, whether mechanical or chemical, whereby copies may be multiplied indefinitely:

"Print," when used to designate a work to which copyright is annexed, shall mean any engraving, woodcut, etching, lithograph, chromo-lithograph, oleograph, map, chart, or plan which is produced and copies of which can be multiplied by any method of impression, whether from stone, metal-plates, wood-blocks, or other material:

"Publication" shall have the following meanings,—

In the case of books, prints, and photographs, the first act

of offering for sale, or advertising, notifying, or exposing
as ready for sale to the public any copy of a work, or
sending any copy of a work to be registered in the
manner provided in this Act :

The " date of publication " shall mean the date of the day
on which the act which constitutes publication took
place :

" Replica " shall mean a repetition of a painting by the same
hand, in the same material, and of or so nearly of the same
size, as to render doubtful the identity of the original work :

" Sale," where applied to a painting or a work of sculpture,
but not when applied to a photograph, shall include the
execution of a work for and by order of a person to whom
the work is to belong for a valuable consideration :

" Sculpture " shall mean and include any statue, model, copy,
or cast carved or made in solid form, either in the round,
in relief, or in intaglio, of any material, and by any process,
though made for and applied to the decoration of any
article of manufacture :

Copyright in Artistic Works.

7. After the commencement of this Act the following
persons and their assigns, whether British subjects or aliens,
shall, after publication, and when required by this Act registration of their respective works, become and be entitled to copyright therein, and if the works consist of musical compositions
or dramatic works, to performing rights also, throughout the
British dominions, provided such works shall have been first
published, or in the case of musical compositions and dramatic
works first published or first performed in public in some part of
the British dominions ; that is to say,

In the case of prints, the person who designs and engraves,
or engraves from the design of another, any original
print on the plate, stone, wood, or other substance
from which copies of the print are to be taken, printed,
or made :

In the case of photographs, the person who takes the
negative of any original photograph.

8. Every author of any original painting or work of sculpture
which shall be made after, or which shall have been made but

shall not have been sold or disposed of before the commencement of this Act, if the author be a British subject, and every author of any such painting or work of sculpture sold by him after the commencement of this Act in the British dominions, if such author be an alien, shall have copyright therein.

9. If any work for which copyright or performing right is given by this Act be written, composed, made, engraved, etched, carved, taken, or painted by two or more persons jointly, the copyright and performing right therein shall in the absence of any agreement belong to such persons jointly, unless one or more of such persons be a pupil or pupils of the other of such persons, in which case the copyright shall belong to the said other person, and no one of such persons shall be deemed to be the owner of the copyright or performing right in any particular part of the work to the exclusion of the other or others, and in the event of the death of any one or more of such joint owners, his or their interest shall vest in the person or persons who would be entitled to any copyright or performing right in any work in which he or they were solely interested jointly with the survivor or survivors ; but this provision shall not be construed as giving a joint copyright in the words and the music of operas, oratorios, cantatas, songs, or other musical compositions of which the words and music are written and composed respectively by different persons.

10. In the case of any article, essay, poem, musical composition, dramatic work, print, photograph, or other work first published in and forming part of any collective work, for the writing, composition, or making of which the author, composer, or maker has been paid by the owner of the collective work, the copyright and performing right shall in the absence of any agreement to the contrary belong to the owner of the collective work and his assigns, and, except in the case of encyclopædias on separate publication by the author, composer, or maker of the same, after the time at which separate publication is authorised by this Act, the copyright and performing right in such article, essay, poem, musical composition, dramatic work, print, photograph, or other work as a separate publication, shall belong to the author, composer, or maker thereof.

12. If any person employs another to make or engrave any print for him, or as his assistant, servant, or workman to work for him for salary, wages, or hire for the purpose of executing, making,

or taking, or assisting in executing, making, or taking prints or photographs, the copyright in such prints or photographs shall belong to the employer.

13. If the person above specified as being entitled to copyright or performing right in their respective works be British subjects, and first publish their works out of the British dominions, they shall not be prevented by such publication from obtaining copyright and performing right in the British dominions, but if within *three years* from such first publication they re-publish such works within the British dominions, they shall respectively be entitled to copyright and performing right therein throughout the British dominions as fully as if they had first published their works in such dominions.

16. No person who makes a print or takes a photograph from a painting or other work shall be deprived of copyright in his own work as a print or photograph by the fact of copyright in the painting or other work, or in the design thereof, belonging to another person, if, before commencing the print or taking the photograph, he has obtained the consent in writing of the owner of the copyright in the painting or other work copied.

17. If any work for which copyright or performing right is given by this Act be first published after the death of the author, composer, engraver, photographer, maker, or other person who would have been entitled to copyright, and, in the case of a musical composition or dramatic work, to performing right therein, if the work had been published by him in his lifetime, the copyright and performing right shall belong in the case of a book, musical composition, dramatic work, or lecture to the owner of the manuscript, in the case of a print to the owner of the plate, stone, or other thing on which the design is engraved, and, in the case of a photograph, to the owner of the negative.

18. In all cases in which copyright or performing right is given by this Act such rights shall respectively be deemed to be of the kind known in England as personal property and in Scotland as moveable estate, and shall be respectively capable of assignment and of transmission by operation of law as such.

Registration.

19. Copyright Registration Office to be established.
20. Registrar of Copyright to be appointed.

21. Assistant registrars may be appointed.

22. Registrars to be under the Board of Trade.

23. Appointment and dismissal of clerks and other persons.

*24. Salaries of registrars and other persons. Fees received
    to be paid into the exchequer.*

26. When any work or copyright or performing right is to be registered, the publisher of the work or the owner of the copyright or performing right, as the case may be, shall send to or deliver at the Copyright Registration Office a request, in such form as may be prescribed, that the same may be registered, and any person requesting registration shall supply, in forms to be provided for that purpose, any information which may be required by any rules made for that purpose under the provisions of this Act, and if the work to be registered be one of which a copy is required by this Act to be delivered for the use of the British Museum, such copy shall be delivered when registration is requested.

27. Every form of request for registration under this Act shall be supplied free of charge to any person requiring it, and there shall be upon every such form a declaration to the effect that all the particulars entered on the form of request for registration by the person signing the same are believed by him to be true, and any person before applying for registration shall sign the declaration, and on delivery of the form at the office for registration the person who has so signed the form of declaration shall be deemed to make a solemn declaration that the particulars entered on the form of request for registration are believed by him to be true, and any person who shall wilfully and corruptly make and subscribe such declaration, knowing the particulars entered on the form of request for registration to be untrue in any material particular, shall be deemed guilty of a misdemeanour, and shall be liable to imprisonment, with or without hard labour, for any term not exceeding *two years*.

28. There shall be paid to the registrar at the said office when any request for registration is made a fee of *one shilling*, the payment of which fee shall be denoted on the form of request for registration by a stamp.

29. Immediately on receiving the form of request for registration of the copyright or performing right with the declaration appended duly signed, and the said fee, and, if required by this Act, a copy of the work to be registered, or as soon after as con-

K

veniently can be the particulars given in the form of request for registration shall be registered, and a certificate shall be given to the person who has requested registration, to be called "The Certificate of Registration of Copyright," which shall be a copy on parchment or some other durable substance of the entry in the register sealed with an official seal of the registrar, which seal shall be provided for that and other purposes, and shall be taken judicial notice of in all courts of law without proof. If the copyright or performing right as the case may be, cannot be conveniently registered and the certificate of registration of copyright granted immediately, a receipt in writing for the same shall be immediately given to the person delivering the said work, form, and fee ; and the certificate of registration of copyright or performing right, as the case may be, shall be dated as of the day on which request was made, and shall be forwarded by post or otherwise to the person entitled thereto or his agent, at an address in the United Kingdom, to be given for that purpose as soon as it is ready for delivery free of further charge to such person, and the registration shall be deemed to have been made on the day on which the request was made.

30. If any person who is preparing for publication a work which will after publication be a subject for copyright or performing right under the provisions of this Act desires to secure the work from being copied, represented, or otherwise dealt with, and to secure for himself on publication the same protection until he can register the work as if the work had been registered immediately after publication, he may before publication give notice to the Registrar of Copyright, in a form which it shall be the duty of the registrar to supply free of charge, that the work is in preparation, and that on or as soon after publication as conveniently can be it is his intention to register the work under this Act, and that he desires that the work may be provisionally registered, and thereupon and upon receipt of a fee of *one shilling* from the applicant, the registrar shall provisionally register the work in a book to be kept for the purpose, to be called "The Provisional Register of Copyright," and shall give to the person making the request a certificate, to be called a "Certificate of Provisional Registration of Copyright," and thereupon the applicant shall for *one month* from the date of publication, if the work be published in the United Kingdom, or for *six months* if published in any other part of the British dominions, have the

same protection for his work when published, and the same rights and remedies if his work be copied, publicly performed, or otherwise dealt with without his consent, as if the work had been duly registered under this Act immediately after publication.

32. Subject to any rules which may be made by the Registrar of Copyright, any person may, on payment to the registrar of a fee of *one shilling*, and making a request in writing in a form to be provided by the registrar for that purpose, require search to be made in the register, by the registrar or other officer of the Copyright Registration Office, to ascertain whether any work in respect of which copyright or performing right might be registered has been registered or provisionally registered, or for any subsequent entry in the register, and search shall be made accordingly ; and if any entry sought for be found, it shall be lawful for the person who has paid the fee to inspect the entry in the book, but not to make any copy thereof or to take extracts therefrom ; and if search for or inspection of more than one entry be required, a separate request in writing shall be made, and a separate fee of *one shilling* paid, for each entry for which search or inspection is required.

33. Any person who requires a copy of any entry in the register or provisional register of copyright shall have a right to obtain one on making written application at the Copyright Registration Office in a form to be kept at that office for the purpose, and it shall be the duty of the Registrar of Copyright to supply such copy, sealed with the official seal, on payment of a fee of *one shilling* for each copy of an entry required. Such copies shall be called "Office Copies."

34. *Registry books not to be produced in court, but certificates of registration and office copies to be received in evidence.*

35. Any person who shall produce or cause to be tendered in evidence any document falsely purporting to be a certificate of registration or provisional registration, or an office copy of an entry in the register, knowing such document to be false, or shall, with fraudulent intent, alter any certificate of registration, shall be guilty of a misdemeanour, and shall be liable to be imprisoned, with or without hard labour, for any term not exceeding *two years*.

36. If any person shall deem himself aggrieved by any entry in the register of copyright, such person may apply, in the manner

hereafter specified, for the rectification of the register by order of a judge or of the Supreme Court of Judicature, and if any order be made it shall be deemed to be a part of such order, whether it be specified in such order or not, that every certificate of registration of copyright is to be delivered up by any person in possession thereof, and on whom a copy of the order is served, to the person who has obtained such order and serves a copy, and such person shall deliver up any such certificate at a Copyright Registration Office to be cancelled or destroyed.

37. *Mode of obtaining rectification of register.*

38. *All copyrights and performing rights to be registered hereafter at the Copyright Registration Office.*

39. And whereas it is desirable that provision should be made with reference to the registry of copyright kept at the Hall of the Stationers' Company, and the registrar appointed by the said company under the powers given in the Act passed in the fifth and sixth years of Her Majesty's reign, and intituled "An Act to amend the Law of Copyright," and under other Acts of Parliament ; and whereas this Act does not affect any book or other work published before or any copyright in existence at the commencement of this Act, but the same remain under the law in force at the commencement of this Act, and it is necessary for the purposes of such works and copyrights that the said registry should be maintained ; and whereas the income derived from the fees and payments for and in respect of registration of copyright, inspection of and search in the said register, and otherwise, will in all probability be materially diminished after the commencement of this Act, *and it is desirable to make provision for the adequate remuneration of the present registrar, and for granting him a pension on retirement from his office :* Be it enacted as long as the present registrar shall continue to hold his office, the registry of copyright directed to be kept at the Hall of the Stationers' Company by the said Acts shall continue to be kept there for the purposes specified in the said Acts, and the present officer shall, subject to any existing power of removal, continue to be the registrar, *and there shall be paid to him so long as he shall continue to hold the said office, out of moneys to be provided by Parliament, such a sum annually as shall be required, in addition to the fees and payments under the said Acts, to make up an income of one thousand pounds, and if he shall retire from the said office there shall be paid to him so long as he shall live,*

out of moneys to be provided by Parliament, a pension or sum of six hundred pounds per annum.

40. Removal of register from Stationers' Hall on death or resignation of present registrar.

Duration of Copyright.

41. Copyright in every book, musical composition, dramatic work, lecture, print, and photograph, and performing right in every musical composition and dramatic work, shall endure for the term of *fifty years* from the date of registration of such work.

42. In the case of any article, essay, poem, musical composition, dramatic work, print, photograph, or other work first published in and forming part of any collective work for the writing, composition, or making of which the author, composer, maker, photographer, or other producer shall have been paid or shall be entitled to be paid by the owner of the collective work, the copyright shall endure for the term of *fifty* years from the date of the registration of the collective work ; but except in the case when any such article, essay, poem, musical composition, dramatic work, print, photograph, or other work is first published in an encyclopædia, the author, composer, maker, photographer, or other producer thereof shall, after *three years* from the date of publication of the collective work, without prejudice to the copyright of the owner of the collective work as against other persons, have a right to publish the article, essay, poem, musical composition, dramatic work, print, photograph, or other work in a separate form, and on registration of such separate publication shall have copyright in such work as a separate publication for the residue of such term of fifty years ; but neither during the said term of three years or afterwards shall the said owner of the collective work publish any such article, essay, poem, musical composition, dramatic work, print, photograph, or other work, or any part thereof, separately, without the consent in writing of the said author, composer, maker, photographer, or other producer thereof.

43. If at the expiration of the said term of fifty years the author of any work shall be still living, and shall not have assigned his copyright therein, it shall be lawful for him to apply to Her Majesty's Privy Council for an extension of the

term of his said copyright, and the Judicial Committee of Her Majesty's Privy Council may, if it be deemed just and reasonable, grant to the said author an extension of the said term for such further time as the said Judicial Committee may think fit; and the said author shall cause the said extension of the said term to be registered at the Copyright Registration Office.

44. Copyright in every original painting and work of sculpture shall endure for the life of the painter or sculptor, and for *thirty years* after his death, and in the case of any such work executed by and belonging to two or more persons jointly, the copyright therein shall endure for the life of the longest liver, and for *thirty years* after his death.

45. If any work in which copyright or performing right is to endure for fifty years from the date of registration shall be published in any British possession in which a register of copyright is kept under any local law, and the author, composer, maker, photographer, or other producer of any work has in the manner permitted by this Act registered the same in such register, and not at the Copyright Registration Office in London, the copyright in such work shall endure for *fifty years* from the date of such registration.

Assignment and Sales.

46. After the commencement of this Act no assignment of copyright or performing right registered at the Copyright Registration Office established under this Act, other than an assignment by operation of law, in any book, or in any article, essay, poem, musical composition, dramatic work, print, photograph, or other work published in a collective work, or in any musical composition, dramatic work, lecture, print, or photograph, or of performing right in any musical composition or dramatic work, shall be effected otherwise than by means of the register; and whenever any assignment by operation of law shall take place; the person in whom the copyright or performing right has become vested shall cause the assignment to be registered, and until it is registered he shall be incapable of assigning such rights.

47. If copyright in any painting or work of sculpture has not been registered, every assignment thereof other than an assignment by operation of law, and any license to copy such

works, shall be by some memorandum in writing signed by the proprietor of the copyright; but if the copyright has been registered, every assignment thereof other than an assignment by operation of law may be effected by means of the register or by memorandum in writing.

48. Whenever after the passing of this Act any painting or work of sculpture shall be sold, or any photograph shall be sold or executed on commission, the copyright shall not in the absence of any agreement to the contrary vest in the purchaser or person for whom the work is executed, but shall remain the property of the painter, sculptor, or owner of the negative of the photograph respectively; and if any painting, work of sculpture, or photograph be first sold after the death of the painter, sculptor, or photographer, the copyright shall not vest in the purchaser, but shall remain the property of the person selling the painting, work of sculpture, or negative of the photograph.

49. When any registered copyright or performing right is to be assigned, the registered owner and the person to whom the assignment is to be made shall sign an agreement, and shall state in a form to be called a " Form of Assignment," forms for which the Registrar of Copyright shall supply free of charge the reference in the register to the copyright or performing right to be assigned, and such other particulars as shall be required by any rules to be made in pursuance of this Act; and there shall be upon the form of assignment a form of request for registration of the copyright or performing right in the name of the person to whom it is assigned, and a form of declaration to the effect that the person assigning has good right to assign, and any person who shall wilfully and corruptly make and subscribe such declaration knowing the same to be untrue in any material particular shall be deemed guilty of a misdemeanour, and shall be liable to imprisonment with or without hard labour for any period not exceeding *two years.*

50. When a form of assignment has been duly signed as required by this Act it shall be delivered at the Copyright Registration Office together with the certificate of registration of copyright or performing right previously issued, unless the same has been lost or destroyed, and there shall be paid to the Registrar of Copyright a fee of *one shilling,* and the same shall be registered and a new certificate or new certificates of registration shall be given to the newly registered owner or owners

of the copyright and performing right respectively, or in case the registration cannot conveniently be effected and the certificate or certificates issued at once a receipt for the form of assignment, and the fee shall be given and the certificate or certificates of registration shall be forwarded free of charge, by post or otherwise, to the newly registered owner or owners. Such assignment so registered shall be effectual in law to all intents and for all purposes whatever as an assignment of the copyright or performing right mentioned therein without being subject to any stamp duty or charge except the said fee of *one shilling*. And when any assignment by operation of law is to be registered, the person entitled to the copyright or performing right and to have the assignment registered shall fill up a form of request for registration, and shall make a declaration to the effect that he has become entitled to the copyright or performing right, and shall state the means whereby he has become so entitled, and the registrar, on receiving the request with a fee of *one shilling* and the certificate of registration, shall register the assignment and grant a new certificate of registration in the same way as if the assignment had been effected by agreement.

51. In the event of an author, composer, engraver, photographer, or maker of a work which is capable of being the subject of copyright or performing right, and in which by the terms of this Act copyright or performing right is to endure for fifty years from registration, dying, becoming bankrupt, or in the case of a woman marrying after having published such work, but before registering it, the right to register, and thereby to secure copyright or performing right, shall pass as personal property, or in Scotland as movable estate, to the person in whom copyright or performing right in the work would have vested if the work had been registered; and such person shall have the same right to register the work, and thereby secure copyright or performing right therein, as the author, composer, engraver, photographer, or maker of the work.

54. In the event of an assignment of a work published and registered anonymously, or in a fictitious name, the publisher whose name is registered shall alone be recognised for all the purposes of the register as the owner of the copyright, and he, or his executors or administrators if he be dead, shall alone be entitled to make the agreement for assignment, and to sign the declaration therein, and to make the assignment.

Infringement ; Remedies and Penalties.

56. The following acts by any other person than the owner, and without his consent, shall be deemed to be infringements of copyright, and, in the case of musical compositions or dramatic works, of performing rights respectively, unless such acts shall be specially permitted by the terms of this or some other Act not hereby repealed.

> In the case of paintings and works of sculpture, prints, and photographs, by repeating, copying, colourably imitating, or otherwise multiplying, or causing or procuring to be repeated, copied, colourably imitated, or otherwise multiplied for sale or hire any such work, or any part thereof, or the design thereof, by any means, in any material, and of any size, and either in or by the same or any other class of work or kind of art as or than that in and by which the original work was executed, or importing or exporting any such repetition, copy, or imitation, knowing it to have been unlawfully made, or importing any such repetition, copy, or imitation, knowing it to have been made in a foreign State, or, knowing any such repetition, copy, or imitation to have been so made, imported, or exported, exhibiting, selling, exposing or offering for sale, distributing, or causing or permitting exhibition, sale, exposure, or offer for sale or distribution thereof.

59. Copyright in any painting, print, or photograph shall not prejudice the right of any person to represent by painting or otherwise the same scene or object represented in the painting, print, or photograph in which the copyright exists, and to obtain copyright in his work.

60. If the owner of copyright or performing right in any work should give permission to any other person to copy, imitate, publicly perform, print, photograph, cast, deliver, or otherwise repeat his work, such permission shall not, in the absence of an agreement to the contrary, disentitle such owner of the copyright or performing right from giving a similar or any other permission to any other person, even though the first person to whom such permission was given may have acquired copyright in his work.

61. If a painting, work of sculpture, print, or photograph, in

which there is copyright, happens to be an object in any scene, the copying of such painting, drawing, work of sculpture, print, or photograph, merely as forming part of the scene, shall not be deemed to be any infringement of the copyright therein, unless the special purpose for which the scene is copied is the exhibition of the copy of the copyright work.

62. If after the commencement of this Act any person shall be guilty of infringing copyright or performing right, the owner of the copyright or performing right shall, in addition to any other remedy, be entitled to maintain an action or other proceeding allowed by the law of the place where the wrong has been committed for damages and for an injunction, or either of them.

64. All copies or colourable imitations of any work in which there is copyright unlawfully made in the British dominions, or unlawfully imported thereinto, shall be deemed to be the property of the owner of the copyright therein respectively, and he shall, in addition to damages for infringement of copyright, and an injunction, or either of them, be entitled, after demand for them in writing signed by him or his agent, to recover them by action, with damages for their detention.

65. And whereas a more summary remedy than an action is frequently required to enable an owner of copyright to recover possession of unlawful copies or colourable imitations of his work, and a power to search for and to seize such unlawful copies or colourable imitations, whether in a house or other building, or when being hawked and carried about for sale, is needed: Be it enacted that upon proof, on the oath of one credible witness before any two justices of the peace, court, sheriff, or other person having jurisdiction in summary proceedings in that part of the British dominions where the offence is committed, that there is reasonable cause to suspect that any person has in his possession, or in any house, shop, or other place, for sale or hire, any copy, repetition, or imitation of any work wherein or in the design whereof there is copyright under this Act, and that such copy, repetition, or imitation has been made without the consent in writing of the owner or any previous owner of the copyright, it shall be lawful for such justices, court, sheriff, or other person as aforesaid, before whom any such proceeding is taken, and he is hereby required to grant a warrant for some peace officer or officer of the court to search in the daytime, with or without the

owner of the copyright, such house, shop, or other place, and if any such copy, repetition, or imitation, or any work which may reasonably be suspected to be such, shall be found therein, to bring the same or cause the same to be brought before him, or some other justices of the peace, court, sheriff, or other person as aforesaid, and upon proof that any or every such copy, repetition, or imitation was unlawfully made, and, except in the cases of paintings and works of sculpture, upon production of the certificate of registration, certificate of provisional registration, or an office copy of the entry in the register of copyright, such and every such copy, repetition, or imitation shall be forfeited and delivered up to the owner of the copyright as his property.

66. If any person elsewhere than at his own house, shop, or place of business shall hawk, carry about, offer, or keep for sale or hire any unlawful copy, repetition, or imitation of any work, wherein, or in the design whereof there is copyright under this Act, every such unlawful copy, repetition, or imitation may be seized without warrant by the owner of the copyright, or any peace officer or other person authorized by him, and forthwith taken before any justices of the peace, court, sheriff, or other person having jurisdiction in summary proceedings, and upon proof that such copy, repetition, or imitation was unlawfully made, and, except in the case of paintings and works of sculpture, upon production of the certificate of registration of copyright, certificate of provisional registration, or an office copy of the entry in the register of copyright, such and every such copy, repetition, or imitation shall be forfeited and delivered up to the owner of the copyright as his property.

67. No action, prosecution, or summary or other legal proceeding to enforce any forfeiture or penalty for infringement of copyright or performing right under this Act, except it be for infringement of copyright in a painting or work of sculpture, shall be maintained or maintainable until the work has been registered at the Copyright Registration Office established under this Act, or at a registration office in some British possession, and a certificate of registration has been obtained by the person entitled thereto; and no such person shall, after registering his work, be capable of maintaining any action, prosecution, or summary or other legal proceeding for or in respect of any act or matter, or any copy, repetition, imitation, performance, repre-

sentation of or interference with his work, committed, made, or done before the date of registration of the work, unless such work has been provisionally registered, and such act, matter, copy, imitation, performance, representation, or interference was committed, made, or done during the continuance of the protection afforded by such provisional registration; and if any copies, repetitions, or imitations of the work have been made before registration of the work, and while the work was not protected by provisional registration under this Act, such owner of the copyright or other person shall not be entitled, after registration of the work, to maintain any action for damages, injunction, or other remedy, or any summary proceeding, to stop the circulation or sale of such copies, repetitions, or imitations, or to enforce any forfeiture or penalty in respect thereof.

68. In case of infringement or anticipated infringement of copyright or performing right in any article, essay, poem, musical composition, dramatic work, print, photograph, or other work published in and forming part of any collective work, it shall be lawful for the author, composer, maker, photographer, or other producer of the article, essay, poem, musical composition, dramatic work, print, photograph, or other work, to take legal proceedings for the recovery of damages for any injury to his interest in such works, or for injunction to prevent such infringement or the continuation of such infringement, even though the copyright is the property of the owner of the collective work, and the three years has not elapsed during which he is debarred from publishing his work as a separate publication.

69. And whereas there may be many cases of infringement of copyright or performing right where the damage sustained by the owner of the copyright or performing right is slight, and insufficient to warrant an action : Be it enacted, that it shall be lawful in every case of infringement of copyright or performing right for the owner of the right to apply in a summary manner to any two justices of the peace, court, sheriff, or other person having jurisdiction in summary proceedings in that part of the British dominions where the wrong has been committed, or where the person who has been guilty of the infringement dwells ; and such justices of the peace, court, sheriff, or other person may, if he or they shall think it just, on production of the certificate of registration, or, in the case of paintings and sculpture, on other proof of the title of the applicant, order the person who has been

guilty of the infringement to pay a penalty not exceeding *five pounds*, and all costs and the money so paid shall be given by way of compensation to the owner of the copyright or performing right.

The British Colonial and other Possessions.

70. Nothing in this Act is intended or shall be construed in such a manner as to lessen or derogate from any power at present possessed by the legislative authorities in any British possession to legislate with respect to copyright in that possession, nor in such a manner as to deprive any person in a British possession of any copyright or performing right he may be entitled to or may hereafter acquire in such possession under any law now in force or hereafter to be made in such possession, or to interfere with or lessen such right.

Foreign Works.   Translations and Adaptations.

77. *No fresh Orders in Council to be made under the International Copyright Acts.   Power to Her Majesty to revoke Orders in Council and issue new orders.*

78. *Power for Her Majesty by Order in Council to direct that foreign authors and others shall have copyright and performing right in the British dominions on certain conditions.*

79. *On such Orders in Council being made this Act with certain exceptions to apply to foreign works.*

80. *No Order in Council to have effect unless it states that due protection is secured for British authors.*

81. *Power for Her Majesty to revoke and alter Orders in Council.*

82. *No person to be entitled to copyright or performing right in the British dominions if he has not copyright or performing right in his own country.*

83. *Title of person alleging foreign copyright and performing right to be presumed, and copy of foreign register to be primâ facie evidence.*

94. And whereas it is desirable to prevent fraud as to paintings, sculpture, prints, and photographs, whether there shall be subsisting copyright or not, by false representation as to the painters, sculptors, engravers, photographers, or other persons

by whom any such works were executed, or by other means ; be it enacted that no person shall do or cause to be done any or either of the following Acts ; that is to say,—

No person shall sign or otherwise affix or cause to be signed, or otherwise affixed to or upon any such work, any name, initials, monogram, or mark of or resembling or colourably imitating the name, initials, monogram, or mark of any person who did not make or execute such work or the negative thereof :

No person shall sell, publish, exhibit, or dispose of or offer for sale, exhibition, or distribution any such work having thereon any such name, initials, monogram, or mark, knowing that such name, initials, monogram, or mark are the name, initials, monogram, or mark of any person who did. not make or execute the work :

No person shall dispose of, put off, sell, or offer for sale or cause to be disposed of, sold or offered for sale, any copy or colourable imitation of any such work, whether there shall be subsisting copyright therein or not, as having been made or executed by the author or maker of the original work from which such copy or imitation shall have been taken or imitated, or any print, cast, or photograph purporting to have been copied or taken from the work or design of a particular painter or sculptor, knowing that in truth it was not copied or taken from the work or design of such painter or sculptor :

No person shall sell, publish, exhibit, or dispose of or offer for sale, exhibition, or distribution any such work as having been painted, executed, or made by a particular person, knowing that the same was not painted, executed, or made by such person :

If the author or maker of any such work, made either before or after the passing of this Act, shall have sold or otherwise parted with the possession of such work, and if any alteration shall afterwards be made therein by any other person, no person knowing of such alteration shall be at liberty to sell, publish, or offer for sale such work or any copies thereof as or for the unaltered work of such author or maker.

If any person shall do or cause to be done any of the said Acts, he shall, upon conviction on summary process before any magistrate, or any two justices of the peace, court, sheriff, or

,other person having jurisdiction in summary proceedings, in that part of the British dominions where the person who has committed the offence shall dwell or carry on business, pay to any person who shall be aggrieved a sum of *ten pounds*, and if the prosecutor shall be a person to whom any such fraudulent or altered work shall have been sold, he shall pay a sum in addition to such ten pounds equal to the price paid by such person for such work and all costs of such proceedings.

95. In every case of a conviction under the last preceding section the said work shall be deemed to be the property of the person whose name, initials, monogram, or mark has been fraudulently affixed thereto, or imitated, or who was the author or maker of any work which has been altered, should he be living at the time of the conviction, or to his personal representatives if he be dead, and immediate notice of such conviction shall be given to him by the person obtaining such conviction, if he can be found, and such person shall hold the said work for him and at his disposal, but if he cannot be found, or if he be not living, such person shall as soon as he reasonably can inform the same, or some other magistrate, justice of the peace, court, sheriff, or other person having such jurisdiction, and the said magistrate, justice of the peace, court, sheriff, or other person, shall order some peace officer or officer of the court to destroy the said work, and the work shall be delivered up for the purpose of being destroyed, and if any such person should not give such notice, or within a reasonable time inform such magistrate, justice of the peace, court, sheriff, or other person, he shall be liable on summary conviction to pay a penalty of ten pounds to the Crown.

96. Upon proof on the oath of one credible person, before any two justices of the peace, court, sheriff, or other person, having jurisdiction in summary proceedings, that there is reasonable cause to suspect that any person has in his possession, or in any house, shop, or other place in that part of the British dominions where such justices of the peace, court, sheriff, or other person has jurisdiction, for sale any painting, work of sculpture, print, plate, or stone for printing photograph, or negative of a photograph, which has been marked with the name, initials, monogram, or mark of, or resembling, or colourably imitating the name, initials, monogram, or mark of any person then living who did not execute such work or the negative

thereof, it shall be lawful for such two justices of the peace, court, sheriff, or other person, before whom any such proceeding is taken, and he is hereby required to grant his warrant to search in the daytime such house, shop, or other place, and if any painting, work of sculpture, print, plate, or stone, photograph, or negative of any photograph, be found so marked, or which may be reasonably suspected not to have been the work of the person whose, or the resemblance or imitation of whose name, initials, monogram, or mark it bears be found therein to cause the same to be brought before him, or some other justices of the peace, court, sheriff, or other person having jurisdiction in summary proceedings in that place, and upon proof that any such painting, work of sculpture, print, plate, or stone, photograph, or negative of a photograph, is so marked, the same shall be forfeited and delivered up to the person whose, or the resemblance or imitation of whose name, initials, monogram, or mark it bears, and from thenceforth it shall be his property.

97. Whenever any painting shall have been sold, and the copyright therein shall remain the property of the painter, such painter shall not, without the consent in writing of the purchaser or other owner of the painting, be entitled by reason of his copyright to make any replica of such painting, and if before selling the painting he shall have made any replica, he shall not, without such consent, be entitled to sell, exhibit, or part with the property in such replica.

98. When any painter shall have sold his copyright in a painting, he shall, notwithstanding anything in this Act, be entitled to use again, in the composition of any other work, any sketches or studies made for or used in the composition of such painting, provided that he shall not, by any second use of such sketches and studies, repeat or colourably imitate the design of such painting, and any such painter and his assigns shall be entitled to sell or otherwise dispose of such sketches or studies, and any such use, sale, or disposition shall not be deemed infringement of the copyright in the painting.

99. If the subject of, or if the principal object in, any painting be the portrait of a purchaser of the work, or of any person whose likeness was stipulated in the agreement for the work, the painter or other owner of the copyright shall not, without the consent in writing of the owner for the time being of the work, be entitled by reason of his copyright therein to repeat, copy, or reproduce in any way, or by any kind of art, the said likeness.

100. Whenever any painting or work of sculpture shall have been sold, and the purchaser or other owner thereof shall not be entitled to the copyright, such purchaser or other owner shall nevertheless have the same right, as the owner of the copyright, to apply to any court of justice, in respect of any matter which is by this Act declared to be infringement of copyright, and the said court shall have power to afford to the said purchaser a remedy, either by injunction with damages, or either of them, as if the said purchaser were owner of the copyright.

101. Whenever after the passing of this Act any photographic portrait is executed on commission, it shall be unlawful for the photographer, or other person who owns the copyright, or for any other person, without the consent in writing of the person for whom the work was executed to sell, offer for sale, or exhibit in public in any shop window, or otherwise, any copy of such portrait, and if any such photographer or person shall sell, offer for sale, or so exhibit any such copy, it shall be lawful for the person for whom the work was executed to summon the offender before any two justices of the peace, court, sheriff, or other person having jurisdiction in summary proceedings in that part of the British dominions where the offence is committed, and such justices of the peace, court, sheriff, or other person on being satisfied that such photographer or other person has any copies of such portrait in his possession for sale, or that he has exhibited the same in public, shall make an order upon such photographer or other person to deliver up to the person for whom the portrait was taken all copies in his possession, and if such photographer or other person shall not forthwith deliver up to such person all such copies, or upon proof on the oath of one credible witness that there is reasonable cause to suspect that such photographer or person has not delivered up all such copies which are in any house, shop, or other place belonging to him, it shall be lawful for such justices of the peace, court, sheriff, or other person, and he is hereby required, to grant a warrant for some peace officer or officer of the court to search in the daytime such house, shop, or other place, and if any such copies shall be found therein, to bring the same or cause the same to be brought before him or some other justices of the peace, court, sheriff, or other person as aforesaid, and the same shall be forfeited and delivered up to the person for whom the portrait was taken as his property.

L

ACTS REPEALED.

FIRST SCHEDULE.

Titles of Acts.

An Act for the encouragement of the arts of designing, engraving, and etching historical and other prints by vesting the properties thereof in the inventors and engravers during the time therein mentioned (8 Geo. 2, c. 13).

An Act to amend and render more effectual an Act made in the eighth year of the reign of King George the Second for encouragement of the arts of designing, engraving, and etching historical and other prints; and for vesting in and securing to Jane Hogarth, widow, the property in certain prints (7 Geo. 3, c. 38).

An Act for enabling the two universities in England, the four universities in Scotland, and the several colleges of Eton, Westminster, and Winchester, to hold in perpetuity their copyright in books given or bequeathed to the said universities and colleges for the advancement of useful learning and other purposes of education; and for amending so much of an Act of the eighth year of the reign of Queen Anne as relates to the delivery of books to the warehouse keeper of the Stationers' Company for the use of the several libraries therein mentioned (15 Geo. 3, c 53).

An Act for more effectually securing the property of prints to inventors and engravers by enabling them to sue for and recover penalties in certain cases (17 Geo. 3, c. 57).

An Act to amend and render more effectual an Act of His present Majesty for encouraging the art of making new models and casts of busts and other things therein mentioned, and for giving further encouragement to such arts (54 Geo. 3, c. 56).

An Act to amend the laws relating to dramatic literary property (3 Will. 4, c. 15).

An Act for preventing the publication of lectures without consent (5 & 6 Will. 4, c. 65).

An Act to extend the protection of copyright in prints and engravings to Ireland (6 & 7 Will. 4, c. 59).

An Act to amend the law of copyright (5 & 6 Vic., c. 45).

An Act for amending the law relating to copyright in works of the fine arts, and for repressing the commission of fraud in the production and sale of such works (25 & 26 Vic., c. 68).

An Act to give effect to an Act of the Parliament of the dominion of Canada respecting copyright. *Section* 4 only repealed (38 & 39 Vic., c. 53).

SECOND SCHEDULE.

An Act to amend the law relating to international copyright (7 & 8 Vict., c. 12).

An Act to enable Her Majesty to carry into effect a convention with France on the subject of copyright; to extend and explain the International Copyright Act; and to explain the Acts relating to copyright in engravings. *Repeal not to extend to section* 14 (15 & 16 Vict., c. 12, in part).

An Act to amend the law relating to international copyright (38 Vict., c. 12).

THE END.

Printed by REMINGTON & Co., 134, New Bond Street, W.

www.ingramcontent.com/pod-product-compliance
Lightning Source LLC
Chambersburg PA
CBHW021126020726
47500CB00003B/936